Peace, O River

Peace, O River

Nancy Garden

FARRAR·STRAUS·GIROUX

New York

"Peace," from the *Girl Scout Pocket Songbook*, copyright 1956 by Girl Scouts of the U.S.A.; reprinted by permission. Lyrics from "Bridge over Troubled Water" on page 158, copyright © 1969 by Paul Simon; used by permission

My thanks to Marshall Simonds, Moderator of the Town of Carlisle, Massachusetts, for helping me with town meeting procedures and the wording of warrant articles. Any errors that remain are mine, not his.

And special thanks to Lorelle Paul.

—N.G.

For Margaret Ferguson, with love

Peace

Peace I ask of thee, O River,
Peace, peace, peace.
When I learn to live serenely
Cares will cease.
From the hills I gather courage,
Vision of the day to be.
Strength to lead and faith to follow,
All are given unto me.
Peace I ask of thee, O River,
Peace, peace, peace.

Girl Scout song, by
Glendora Gosling and Viola Wood

Peace, O River

I

SHE COULDN'T WAIT. As soon as the movers left, and after giving only the quickest of glances around her new-old room, Kate thrust her suitcases into her closet, pushed the door to, and scrambled out the window. The Kincaids had lived in this house before, and Kate climbed out the window to see if, after four years of living in a city, she still could.

She did it easily. The wisteria vines outside her window were, if anything, thicker, and Kate was, if anything, stronger at sixteen than she'd been at twelve. Would Jon be?

"Miserable rat!"

That was her brother, Dan, good-naturedly watching her from the front yard. Dan was eighteen, and to her a gentle, overgrown bear, kind and somewhat clumsy.

He accosted her, grinning, as soon as she hit the ground. "How did I know you'd do that?" he asked affectionately, running a hand over the shaggy vine, which still trembled from supporting Kate.

Kate shrugged and grinned back.

"I always envied you," Dan said, "having that vine."

"Go on," said Kate, surprised. "You never needed it. Seems to me you always had permission to go out, especially the last couple of years we were here."

"Sibling rivalry," said Dan cheerfully. "And envy of the male."

Kate punched him and he grabbed her playfully with an arm strong from working their grandfather's corn and squash fields all summer. Then, as they both turned back toward their proper New England house, white clapboard with green shutters, he remarked, "Smaller, isn't it?"

"We're bigger, Dan."

"I know." He let her go. "Also I know you didn't climb down that vine to stand here talking with me. But . . ."

"What?"

He looked away. "I just registered, that's all. Thought I might as well get it over with."

Kate tried to compose a reaction. She'd guessed he would, of course—would register for the draft as soon as they'd moved in. Since he'd just turned eighteen, he "had" to, as far as the law was concerned. Except she knew if she'd been a boy she would have tried to avoid it, and it was the biggest difference between them. Even when they'd been little, he'd always been the one to point out what they should be doing or what wasn't allowed. It wasn't that he was a prig; it was just that his sense of duty sometimes made him do things that even he wasn't sure he believed in. Kate couldn't stomach that, though she tried hard not to let it show.

"Dad'll be pleased, I guess," she said evasively. "That you made up your mind, anyway."

"I didn't *want* to do it, Kate. And"—suddenly he was vehement—"damn it, it's hard in this family to do what's right!" He turned before she could respond with the

4

sympathy she felt, and strode up the steps to the house, slamming the old wood-frame screen door behind him.

Kate heard their mother's voice protesting from inside. In their house in Providence they'd had a metal door with a scaled-down air brake that prevented slams. Poor Mom! Now she'd have to spend summers futilely training them again as she had when they'd been children.

But Kate had to hurry; Jon had said four-thirty last night when he'd called her long distance to arrange when they'd meet.

She went quickly down the front path, remembering to close and latch the gate of the white picket fence behind her.

The tangle of overgrown perennials and weeds in the front garden immediately made Kate visualize her mother there, kneeling, grubbing contentedly in the dirt, a scarf holding her hair back and her garden gloves forgotten on the grass beside her. Maybe Mom'll relax now that she's got her garden back, Kate thought; maybe Dad will, too.

Feeling twelve again and hopeful, Kate ran across the town common, where the good citizens of River View, Massachusetts, had been allowed to graze their sheep and cows back in the early eighteenth century. At the common's far edge, she remembered an obscure ritual she and Jon—Jonathan Westgate—had followed since they'd first gone to school together at the age of six. Happily observing it again, she kicked three times at the tumbled rock cairn that was all that remained of the town pound, which had enclosed eighteenth-century strays till their owners came to claim them.

It wasn't far to the river, along Route 40 out of town; already she could smell it in the early September heat and feel its humidity. She walked faster, the river drawing her as much as Jon; then slowed, familiar sights holding her back. There was the Carter house, bleak and gray and multigabled on its barren hill, overlooking the road like the witch she and Jon had once imagined living there. Later, when they were nine or so, they'd learned firsthand that old Mrs. Carter was indeed witchlike in her treatment of anyone who came up her path, whether mail carrier, paper deliverer, or child seeking lost ball or dog.

Across from Mrs. Carter's house, behind a prickly hedge of pink rugosa roses, was the Wilson place, sunny twig-jumbled yard growing into neatly kept horse pasture. Next came the Wilsons' woods, then conservation land kept free of buildings for everyone's children and grandchildren against the expected time when the still essentially rural town would turn suburb. After that came the big bend in the road; then the gray-shingled cottage that sold ice cream in summer and hot chocolate in winter. You could skate on the pond across the road from the Ice Cream Shack, and she and Jon had, many times, till Jon, who'd never learned to swim, fell through one day and nearly drowned.

Then came the narrowing of the road, near the bridge leading across the river, and the thinning of trees and brush making up the hummocky point that provided the vista for which River View had been named. The point jutted sharply into the water, facing the harborlike negative of itself that had no doubt suggested the name of the town opposite: Hastings Bay. Hastings Bay's houses, poorer than River View's and more often needing paint because of the damp that perpetually invaded them, clustered low on the flood plain, staring silently across.

It was not quite four-thirty. Kate reached the bridge and climbed down the bank to its left, glad to see blueberry bushes and swamp azalea still tangled there, making a transition to where the woods began again a few yards back. The bank dropped quickly to the water, its edge undercut and only sparsely tufted with grass because of so many toes scrambling, so many bottoms sitting. The bushes overhung the bank and crowded together on either side of the small opening that faced Hastings Bay's wide boat-launching strip just opposite —no grass at all there, boat-bottoms, Kate thought, giggling, being harder by far than people-bottoms.

Tee shirt sticking uncomfortably to her thin back in the heat, Kate took off her sandals and rolled up her jeans. She poked at the cool river mud with her big toe, allowing herself at last, in the joy of being back, to feel the pain of her four years away—four years of evenly paved urban streets and perfectly tended lawns, of houses whose brick, stone, and paint were never marred with damp or mildew, whose gardens never went to weeds, and whose orderly, fenced, and hidden vegetable patches were never raided by rabbits or woodchucks. Her school had been a small private one, all girls; there had been no one like Jon to be friends with, for most of the people there seemed stiff and citified compared to those she'd grown up with. Just one, Chelsea Tay, had become sort of a friend because she, unlike the others, Kate decided in her first week there, had thoughts that went deeper than the words of the latest popular song.

I was a snob then, Kate thought, digging her toes deeper into the mud, a country snob, and I never gave them a chance. Now, she thought exultantly, I don't have to; I never have to go back there again. It's not the money itself that's to blame, Kate said to herself— for River View was wealthy enough. But River View hid its affluence behind quiet New England charm instead of flaunting it. Still, across the river in Hastings Bay most people's houses stood on postage-stamp lots, while River View's were surrounded by three or more acres of private land. Snob zoning, some people called it, though others said it was simply intended to keep the town as rural as possible for as long as possible. The same kind of zoning made it difficult for businesses to move in. River View's families shopped in Hastings's supermarkets, since View had only a tiny "convenience" store. River View's lawyers and professors and engineers took their cars to Hastings's mechanics and body shops to be fixed . . .

"Hey, Miss Kettle!"

The familiar voice edged its way around the point, and Kate ran toward it, splashing, yelling, "Hey, Mr. Pot!" The names came from the day back in second grade when Jon had told Miss Argyle, their teacher, that Katy Kincaid had spilled her snack-time milk. Miss Argyle, pointing out the squashed chocolate chip on Jon's shirt, had reprimanded him, saying he was a fine example of "the pot calling the kettle black."

And there he was now, the Pot himself, his tattered cutoffs spotted with mud, his face still freckled, his blond hair tousled, and his snubby nose smudged. He ran to her, splat-splatting into the water, and held her in a huge hug—lord, he had grown taller, though he still was shorter than she, still skinny and frail-looking.

Well, I've grown, too, Kate thought, suddenly self-conscious about breasts and bra, for she'd been nearly as flat as Jon when she'd left.

But Jon didn't seem to notice.

"Christmas, Katy!" he yelled, slapping her on the back. "Miss Kettle, Miss Kettle, I can't believe you're home."

"I'm home," Kate said, a little subdued at his excitement; he might be taller, but he seemed no older, somehow.

"Fishing's not too good anymore," Jon said apologetically. "Neither's frogging, in the spring. People've scared everything wild away. Hastings kids even make bonfires every night now, and party on their boat launch."

"Sounds okay," said Kate, wondering momentarily if he'd become a prude—but no, he couldn't have, not Jon. They were wading along the shore now, upstream and away from both towns, slowly. "Don't View kids do that, too?"

Jon shook his head. "View kids mostly go to the Ice Cream Shack. Last year some kids lit a fire here but the police got nervous and made them put it out. There's not as much open space on our side."

"That's true," Kate agreed.

They walked to their old frogging place, where Jon's bike was stashed with his shoes and fishing gear, and stood there awkwardly, Jon leaning on his handlebars. "You didn't write much," he said.

"No," said Kate. "I'm sorry. I was pretty busy."

"You're a liar," said Jon, and she stopped her protest before it got out, for this was the old Jon again, who'd always seen through her. "You just hate writing."

"Letters," she said quickly. "It's letters I'm no good at. But I still write poems."

He smiled as if he'd known that, too, or guessed it. "Do I get to see any?"

"Maybe." No one had seen her poems, not Chelsea, or Dan, or even her mother. But Jon—he was almost her twin, so his reading them would be like reading them herself. "You still make ship models and play the guitar?" she asked, and he nodded.

For a while they said nothing. Kate scrunched her toes in the mud again and Jon watched, then looked away. "You've filled out some," he said finally.

"You haven't."

"I know. Wish I had."

"You will."

She reached her hand out to him, the tears choking behind her eyes and in her throat, and he touched it below her thumb where the narrow blood-brother scar matched the one beneath his thumb. They hugged again, harder this time, and sadly for all the words they'd missed saying to each other, and all the growing they'd had to do alone.

ᢒᢘ2

WATERY SUNLIGHT slid beneath Kate's window shade early the next morning, puddling the floor with gold. She grunted, punched the snooze button on her clock radio, and snuggled deeper. The floor of her room was a mountain range of still-unpacked cartons and unsorted books. Her suitcases, wrested from her closet the night before in a frantic search for pajamas, were strewn about, open, their lids hanging precariously, ready to bob at the slightest touch.

"Katy!"

"S'okay, Mom, I'm awake."

Her mother opened the door anyway, snorted "Ha!" and strode to the window, snapping the shade up. Kate groaned and closed her eyes tighter. "Looks like rain later," her mother said, sturdy plaid-shirted arms making triangles against slim hips; she had a figure the girls in Providence, especially Chelsea, had envied. Kate had little need to, being equally slender, except on top. "Or one of those days that can't make up its mind. Too bad, on the first day of school." Mrs. Kincaid leaned down and hugged Kate, then sat on the edge of the bed. "Glad to be back?" she asked.

"Umm-hmm. You?"

Her mother sighed. "Glad and hopeful. Daddy already

seems more relaxed. He's out looking for our old vegetable garden in the weeds." She stood up, stretching. "Have you *seen* the weeds out back? Tall as the house, some of them."

Kate chuckled; her mother's exaggerations were a family joke. "Better rent a cherry picker then, so you can get above them to pull them out." She threw off the covers and got out of bed. Her mother stared at her and then laughed, pointing. "What's the matter?" Kate asked, and then looked down and laughed herself, for she had on a red-and-white-striped pajama top and blue bottoms. "The latest thing," she said, doing a clumsy pirouette. "Don't you like it?"

"Oh, yes," said her mother. "It's definitely you— what they're wearing in Paris, I suppose?"

"In Paris," said Kate, stripping off her pajama top and reaching for her clothes, "they aren't wearing anything at all."

With another laugh, her mother blew her a kiss and left, closing the door softly.

It took Kate a good ten minutes to find the shoes she wanted to wear, another five to find her brush and run it through her nearly shoulder-length brown hair, straight as Dan's but, as her mother said, "thank-heaven-thicker." She should have asked Jon what people wore to school—she'd had to wear a uniform in Providence —but Massachusetts, she thought, can't be all that different from Rhode Island. Public school kids there wear normal everyday clothes, so they must here, too. Thank goodness, thought Kate, glancing at her jeans and shirt in the full-length mirror that had somehow found its way to the wall next to her closet. No more blue plaid skirt, no more blazer—Saturday every day of the week, at least as far as clothes go!

The upstairs hall and the landing at the top of the two steps leading to Dan's room were covered with labeled cartons: BATHROOM, DAD'S STUDY, SEWING STUFF, BOOKS, BOOKS, BOOKS, BOOKS . . . We probably have more books than any other family in River View, Kate thought cheerfully as she ran down the stairs; more than any library, more than Brown, more than Harvard . . .

The kitchen was in even worse chaos than the rest of the house, except maybe Kate's room. Partly unpacked cartons, most of them huge cardboard dish "barrels," crowded each corner, and odds and ends of equipment —pots, cookie sheets, dish towels—perched on nearly every flat surface. Kate took an egg beater off what she assumed would be her chair and sat down at the round table in the center of the room.

"I'm not at all sure," said Mom from the stove, where she was frying bacon, "that that's where the table goes."

Kate reached for the toast that had just sprung out of the toaster. "I thought you made a floor plan," she said. Her mother had been a theatrical set designer before she'd had Dan, and still prided herself on her scale drawings.

"I did," said Mom, "but I've either temporarily lost my touch or changed my mind. It looks terrible there, don't you think?"

"Not terrible," said Kate, "just crowded. You got the butter?"

Her mother tossed her a partly wrapped stick from the side of the stove.

"Thanks," said Kate. "I mean, do you visualize these

cartons as an essential part of the decor? If so, then yes, definitely crowded. If not, then . . ."

"Bacon!" Kate's father, wearing an old battered hat and reeking of insecticide, clumped in his work boots up the back steps and into the kitchen, slamming the screen door.

"*How* many times . . ." began Mom.

". . . do I have to tell you not to slam the door," finished Kate and her father in chorus.

"How's the garden?" asked Kate, underneath really asking *how are you?* She scanned her father's face as she did every morning, searching for new tension lines, old worries lurking behind his eyes.

But he seemed fine.

"The Amazon jungle has nothing on it," he said, reaching for toast and spreading it with the low-cholesterol margarine that was waiting beside his plate. "I guess the Pringles just weren't 'into' gardening, as the saying goes, but you'd think they'd have done *something* out there, planted grass seed or shrubs or something."

The Pringles were the people who'd bought the Kincaids' house four years earlier when Kate's father had gotten the job as head of the history department at Brown University, necessitating the move to Providence. Luckily, they'd been ready to move on and willing to sell the house back to the Kincaids when Dad had had his heart attack and had to take early retirement.

"The Pringles," said Mom, putting three and a half strips of bacon on Kate's plate, two and a half on her own, and one on her husband's, "had brown thumbs. And forefingers, and ring fingers, and pinkies, et cetera. Look at the perennial bed in the front. I can't even *find* the bluebells. The day lilies have taken over everything."

"And it's only around two months till the first frost date, less if the weather here's as unpredictable as it used to be," said Dad, putting his hand—still thin, Kate saw with a pang; pale in comparison to Mom's and even her own—on his wife's hand. "What a pity."

"Isn't it?" said Mrs. Kincaid, her eyes sparkling. "Oh, Jim, I'm so glad we're back!"

"Me, too."

"Are you? No regrets?"

"The only regret," he said, "is what we all went through last June." He took Kate's hand, too, briefly, and squeezed it.

"It's over, Daddy," she said.

June was when she'd come home from school early one day and found him motionless on the floor; when she had somehow remembered her CPR training and had bent over him for an interminable twenty minutes, breathing her breath into his lungs and making her hands force his heart to pump, till her mother had come home and the medical technicians from the ambulance she'd quickly called had brushed her aside.

"It's an ill wind," said Mrs. Kincaid briskly, clearly trying, as she'd done many times before, to keep them all from thinking too much about that day and the terrifying ones that had followed. "Life's going to be much nicer from now on. We'll see more of each other, do more things, get to know the community again."

"Speaking of the community," said Dad, delicately nibbling the little bit of bacon he was allowed to have, "think I'll take a walk—get that, Julie, walk?" Mom nodded; he was supposed to walk four or five miles a day.

"—down to Claret's store after breakfast, see if the town paper's still being published . . ."

"Hey, maybe you could write for them," Kate interrupted, excited at the idea. "Weren't they always looking for reporters?"

"Maybe I could," he replied thoughtfully. "Although I was sort of thinking of offering my services to the historic commission."

"One thing at a time, Jim," Mom said softly.

"Right." Dad looked around. "And speaking of our seeing more of each other as a family," he said, "seems to me I haven't seen Dan since sometime last night."

"Sound asleep," said Mom, pouring coffee, decaffeinated for Dad, real for herself and Kate. "I told him that at the rate he's sleeping his mornings away, when he goes in to Cambridge this week to register at school he'd better limit himself to afternoon classes."

"Lazy cur," said Dad mildly, but Kate knew he was proud of Dan and pleased he was going to start college this fall. He was openly pleased it was Harvard, but Kate was sure Dad was also glad that for the next four years college would probably keep Dan from joining the army —even though last night Dad had been supportive when Dan announced he'd signed up for the draft. "No point in courting a jail sentence," Dad had said. But Kate had noticed he watched Mom as he said it. Mrs. Kincaid had been brought up a Quaker, and although she had never tried to mold her children to her beliefs, Kate knew she had hoped Dan would be a conscientious objector.

As for me, thought Kate, pushing back her chair to leave for school, I'm glad women don't have to register yet, so I don't have to risk going to jail.

. . .

Jon's house was on River Road, which followed the river up- and downstream from the bridge, making the top part of a T to Route 40's stem and eventually, on its downstream end, passing the River View/Hastings Bay Regional High School. Kate biked along Route 40 in the hazy morning, noticing that there seemed to be more commuters' cars than she remembered. Still, there was far less traffic than in Providence, and less rush.

The mist was low over the river when she reached the point and she stopped a moment, watching the current's easy flow and ignoring the cars whirring over the bridge on their way east to Cambridge and Boston. Someone was on the boat launch on the Hastings Bay side, shoving off a rowboat with an outboard motor tilted on its stern. For a moment she envied him. First-day-of-school and first-real-day-back jitters were already making her mouth dry and her palms uncomfortably damp.

She wondered which of her old classmates would be there, whom she'd remember, what they would be like. Some of them, Jon had told her yesterday, had moved away. Others had switched to private schools, and one, a pudgy girl named Gilda, whom Kate had never liked but who'd been very popular, had been killed in an automobile accident just last spring.

But this, Kate thought, watching the quiet brown water, never changes, not the river.

"Dreaming?"

It was Jon, coming up silently beside her, watching the current with her before she even knew he was there.

"The river," said Kate, "is never any different."

"I know. It's the one true thing. Scared?"

"A bit. Not scared, really. Nervous."

"All the kids are curious about you. But it'll be okay. They all liked you four years ago, after all. Sixth-grade president, founder of the poetry club."

Kate laughed. "That's just because I was so bossy. They mixed that up with being competent."

Jon's eyes were mischievous. "Are you still?"

"Bossy Kate?" she asked, using the usually-but-not-always-friendly nickname that had followed her through elementary school. "I don't know. Hey," she said, to change the subject, "how come you came back this way?" Jon's house was ahead of them, closer to school than Kate's or the bridge.

He pointed to his watch. "Thought you'd gotten lost, you took so long," he said. "Now—Miss Kettle." He hopped on his bike, then offered her his arm in the old way they'd had of riding arm in arm, bike next to bike —or trying to.

It didn't work any better than it ever had, for despite Jon's new tallness he still had trouble reaching her, which threw them both off balance.

"I still have to catch up to you," he said wistfully. "Remember that summer before you left? We could just about do it then."

"We will again," she said. "You'll grow more, and I won't."

"I'd better." He gave her shoulder a quick pat and then turned out onto the road, pedaling fast.

She turned out after him, and soon caught up.

River Road, once it left the hilly point and turned, flattened out as if stretching itself, and rolled smoothly along the widest part of the river, so close you could smell the water's weedy freshness. The river became deep and still here, right before the school, in the summer thick with lily pads and chuggarumming frogs. At the school itself, it narrowed, its banks pulling together and its current quickening, in the spring often overflowing in its haste to fit through the narrow passage beyond the school where it began the last run of its long journey to the sea.

The sun made the haze translucent to the east as Kate and Jon pulled into the flat tar driveway—newly oiled, Kate noticed—and pedaled up to the sprawling red brick school. Kate's throat tightened when she saw the way the students who were clustered outside, in the parking lot and by the bike stands, stopped talking and watched her ride up.

3

UNLIKE THE HOUSES in town, the regional high school building seemed bigger than Kate remembered. She'd never been close up to it, though, so she wasn't surprised that it had shrunk in her memory. But her classmates! It was so odd to see them grown that she almost laughed. Then, as she got off her bike and walked toward them, she realized that they must remember her as twelve years old, too, and be just as startled.

"Kate?" A tall girl, with yellow hair wisping around her face, detached herself from the group. She came toward Kate, holding out her hands.

"I don't believe it!" Kate exclaimed. "Marcia? Marcia Brooks!" and they hugged, squealing, for they'd been seatmates in fifth and sixth grades, not exactly friends but certainly more than acquaintances.

"I don't believe it either," said Marcia, tossing her hair back and putting an arm around Kate's waist, leading her away from Jon and toward the group. She stopped, looking into Kate's face, laughing. "I expected you to be shorter, with pigtails and braces and that awful blue skirt you used to wear with the elephant on it, remember?"

"Oh, good grief, yes!" Corduroy, it had been, and the elephant had one spangle for an eye. She'd hated it by the end of the year but her mother had sometimes made her wear it on cool days because it was the only in-between skirt Kate had picked out when they'd gone shopping. "And your fuzzy sweater . . ."

"Angora!" shouted Marcia. "It got all over everything."

"It got all over *me*, you mean," said Kate, tears coming from the laughter, "that time we had the fight over —over what?"

"Whose pen," said Marcia. "Remember we both had the same black pen and we got them mixed up and one got lost or something—oh, Kate!" She hugged her again. "It's *good* to see you."

"It's good to be back," said Kate, and then, suddenly stiff, with Jon standing quietly in the background, she faced the others.

Some were new. The first girl who stepped forward was as tall as Marcia but with neater blond hair and a face, Kate thought, that must make boys weak. It turned out she was Carol Somebody—Lodge or Dodge—new two years ago and Marcia's best friend now. There was Becky James, petite and dark and athletic, staccato in her motions like a little quick bird, and several other girls whose names were familiar but who looked like women instead of the sixth graders she remembered them as. The more she saw how they'd changed while at the same time remembering how they'd been, the more Kate felt her own self slipping away; was she twelve now or sixteen?

Then there were the boys, first Charlie Moss, his mouth as small and aristocratic as before, but tucked behind a chin that jutted out more than it used to

—good old Charlie, the class clown and the first boy Kate had ever "liked," who'd rescued her cat once from a dog who'd treed it. Beside him was fat Ricky Jarvis, only he had become stocky and muscular instead of fat, except for his hands; Ricky had pulled her hair long ago because he liked her (said Mom). And there was redheaded Pete Tupp, who'd always taken a lot of teasing because of his name, but who looked, now that his freckles had faded and he'd filled out, as if he could easily give back twice of anything he got. The boys looked enormous; they'd almost all of them been shorter than she when she'd left and now they dwarfed her, making her feel insubstantial. Their voices as they greeted her were men's voices; she hadn't noticed that with Jon, she realized. Then it came to her that his voice had changed along with the others', but had stayed light, a boy's voice hidden beneath a man's. She turned, looking for him, just as he came up to her.

"Still faithful to the end, is Jon," said Becky, smiling and adjusting the sweat shirt she wore draped around her neck and shoulders, its sleeves dangling. "Lord knows I've tried to change that . . ."

The others laughed and pushed at Becky playfully. There are whole traditions now, Kate thought, feeling lonely among them, that I don't know anything about.

A sudden tire screech and squealing of brakes made Kate turn, heart pounding. In Providence that would have meant a hit dog or a barely missed pedestrian more times than not. But it was only a battered black sedan, passenger door dented and wired shut, fenders twisted and flaking rust—no immediate danger to anyone or anything but itself as it screeched around the corner on what seemed like two wheels and came to a momentary stop beside Kate and the others.

A large boy, thick black hair waving over a too-small head, tee-shirt poking out the neck from under faded red plaid, leaned out and brashly looked Kate up and down. Stuck on himself, thought Kate, certain she'd never met him.

"Move it, Skid," said Charlie, once again the protector, stepping in front of Kate.

"Just saying welcome home," said the boy, still eyeing Kate, smiling but in a way no one would call friendly. "Gotta be polite to returning notables, C-boy."

"Get," said Charlie, none too evenly, and the boy, holding up both hands as if in surrender, peeled away into the parking lot.

"Who was that?" asked Kate, astonished as well as disturbed; no one had ever looked at her in quite that way before. "Another new kid?"

"No," said Charlie, "that's Skid Johnson, from Hastings Bay. I understand they started calling him Skid the year he got his first tricycle." Everyone chuckled, but Charlie's face quickly turned serious again. "The big thing you're going to find different in school here, Katy," he said, "is the Hastings kids."

"They can't be that different," Kate said, and then turned to Jon, her discomfort mounting as she saw the others exchange knowing glances.

"I'm glad we were here to meet you," said Marcia, putting her hand on Kate's shoulder for a moment, "because I guess you're going to be a little like we were two years ago when we were freshmen and first met the Hastings Bay kids."

"Only then," said Ricky, "it was worse, 'cause they were waiting for us."

"They're probably waiting for the River View freshmen right now," said Charlie.

"Yeah." Ricky grunted a little as he righted an old three-speed bike that had been lying on its side near him. "We'd better get over there. There's still a good five minutes before the first bell. Come on."

"Nurse detail," said Charlie to Marcia and the other girls. "You coming?" He turned away with Ricky, then looked back, calling, "Just kidding—see you, Katy."

But Kate was shaken nonetheless. "*Nurse* detail?" she asked Jon as the others, waving, followed Charlie.

Jon shrugged. "I don't get involved," he said. "And if you're smart, you won't either."

"Involved in what?" asked Kate, exasperated.

"They're supposed to hate us and we're supposed to hate them," Jon said, stowing his bike and motioning Kate to do the same. "It's all-pervasive, a sort of feud, but, well, dumb."

Kate threaded her front wheel into the bike rack, next to Jon's. "Why dumb?" she asked, thinking that if people like Charlie and Marcia were involved in the "sort of feud" it must have some justification. And Becky— she'd gone off with the others and she'd always been one of the most sensible people in their class.

But Jon put his hand on her arm and said, "We can talk about it later. Let's go in; it's almost time anyway."

It was a long day, punctuated with announcements over a brassy-sounding PA system that made Kate think of futuristic science-fiction novels. She was sure she'd never get used to it; there had been nothing like it in her private school. "Freshmen report to their home rooms," someone had trumpeted when she and Jon entered the vast building that seemed all glass and corridor. "Freshmen report to home rooms." Later, when the upperclassmen were similarly directed and Kate and Jon had found their home room, a different, more military-sounding voice said, "Attention all students. New lockers will be installed by next week. Until then, keep all belongings in home rooms. New lockers are double, so you will have to find locker mates by Friday, or be assigned. Repeat: Find locker mates by Friday or be assigned."

"What was all that?" Kate whispered to Jon, who had managed to sit next to her just as a student teacher began passing out schedule cards as if they were largesse.

"Basement flooded last spring," Jon whispered back as the student teacher obligingly looked the other way. "All the way up to the first floor. So the lockers got all rusty and had to be replaced. Of course they didn't get it done in time."

"Can we be locker mates?"

"I wish. But they're—you know, segregated. Guys and girls. Sorry."

So there was that, too. Through the confusing round of classes, during which everyone except Kate and the bewildered freshmen knew where to go, Kate had to find herself a locker mate. Everyone she asked, all the girls she knew from before, already had them. "Sorry, Katy," Marcia told her. "I wish I'd thought of it; it would have been fun. But Carol Lodge and I already decided." It was the same with Becky, who was sharing with someone named Karen whom Kate hadn't met, and with the others—shrieks and hugs and how-are-you's and wow-have-you-changed's—and then, "Sorry. Darn it, I wish I'd thought!"

I'll find someone by Friday, Kate told herself at the end of the day as she gathered her things together. Or maybe I'll just let myself be assigned; why not?

She put her books on her bike carrier and then, remembering that Friday was also the deadline for signing up for an after-school sport, decided to walk down to the fields and see if anything interesting was going on.

Soccer, of course—she waved at Jon, who was trying out for it—but she'd hated dodge ball in elementary school and soccer had never seemed very different. Field hockey, lacrosse. Kate sighed, wheeling her bike around. There was nothing individual, it seemed, no badminton, no archery, and Marcia had already told her that swimming was full. It didn't even look as if there was tennis, unless there were courts in the back.

Kate leaned her bike against a tree and walked around the far side of the building, from where she could hear excited athletic-sounding shouts, mostly female.

There was a cluster of girls, and a few others standing alone or in pairs, at the side of a long elliptical track around which still others, in green shorts and green and white singlets, loped smoothly and gracefully. Over to one side were three girls practicing broad and high jumps, and Kate found herself holding her breath as one of them vaulted over a bar Kate knew she couldn't even reach with her hands, let alone leap over. She turned back to watch the runners, and thought of her father's track trophy, earned at Harvard, and his saying wistfully earlier in the summer that if he'd kept it up he might never have had his heart attack. I could do that, she said to herself, watching them more closely. I bet I could!

But even as she imagined herself doing it, her muscles froze. At least she'd had some practice at badminton, archery, and swimming—but running? Nothing more formal than a few childhood games of tag and an occasional "race you to the corner" challenge hurled at Jon or Dan. None of the girls she was watching even seemed out of breath. And, she thought, look how thin they are, all over. I'm too top-heavy to do what they're doing.

But the feeling—it must be wonderful, skimming over the ground like that.

"They tell me it hurts like the dickens," said a voice by her side, "but I'm not sure I believe them."

Kate turned to see a short, almost fat girl, her friendly china-doll face framed by a tangle of blond curls. She looked comfortable smiling.

They both watched the girls running around the track. "That one," Kate said, finally finding a runner whose open mouth formed a tense double line—a tall girl with no shape. "The one who looks like a pencil? Look at her face. Something hurts."

"Pencil, that's good." The girl beside her laughed. "What I wouldn't give . . . But you're right. She looks awful. Of course she was already running when the others started. Still, poor kid. I'm glad I'm not an athlete." She took a small bag of potato chips out of her book bag and offered it to Kate.

"Thanks," said Kate, taking a single chip, again conscious of how obviously overweight the girl was.

"Take the whole thing," the girl said, thrusting it at Kate, her wild curls bobbing as if for emphasis. "I know what you're thinking and you're right. Here. You'd be doing me a favor. Really."

"You're not that heavy," said Kate, feeling guilty for being so transparent.

"Oh, yes, I am. Why do you think I'm here watching these sylphs? Envy. I have a love-hate thing with all athletes."

"Well, look," said Kate impulsively, "I was thinking of signing up for track. Only I—I'm not altogether a sylph either, so why don't we both sign up? We could be miserable together."

The girl turned and studied Kate. "You're sure not fat," she said. Then, as if deciding Kate had really meant what she'd offered, she said, "I've got a better idea. Why don't we, you know, work into it gradually? Maybe we could come here early and run by ourselves, before anyone's around to watch. I mean, can you picture me in those cute little shorts they wear?"

"Well . . ." began Kate. "Oh, look, you're not that heavy."

"Second time you've said that. Maybe I'm not, but I'm not getting any thinner either. See, I had hepatitis last spring from eating a bad clam and I had to live on milk and cheese and ice cream and stuff and stay in bed for weeks. A losing battle." The girl giggled. "I guess maybe I should say a gaining one."

"So you're not naturally—overweight?"

"Maybe I'm naturally *plump*, but not naturally gross. I mean, it was always controllable. And I bet you're not naturally, um, top-heavy."

Kate laughed. There was something about this girl that made her feel like saying things she'd never said before. "Look at the Pencil," she commented as the thin girl came around again. "She doesn't have to worry about bouncing up and down as she runs. Now look at me."

The girl stepped back and scrutinized Kate again. "Mmm," she said. "But you're thin everywhere else. Besides, so what? Look at it this way. What guy would go for one of those sticks? Most guys like a woman with some meat on her. That's what my brother says, anyhow, and to hear him talk, he sure oughta know."

"I guess," said Kate evasively; she wasn't sure how she felt about that kind of thing yet.

"Anyway," the girl said, "no one could ever mistake you for anything but a woman, right? But the Pencil there—she might be a tree, or a ten-year-old boy, but a woman? You'd have to look pretty hard and pretty close up to figure that out, right?"

Kate laughed again in spite of herself.

"Of course," continued the girl, "she's probably got a beautiful, very feminine soul. And, oh," she added as the Pencil came around again, "she sure can run! She doesn't even look like she's hurting anymore." She turned to Kate. "How about it?"

"How about what?"

"Us. Coming here early and running. I'm serious."

Kate hesitated, but she couldn't think of any reason not to try it. "Okay," she said. "You're on."

The girl grinned and held out her hand, then slapped Kate's. "Pippa Brown," she said. "Short for Phillippa. I'm a junior. Hi."

"Kate Kincaid." Kate grinned back. "I'm a junior, too."

A car horn blared from the parking lot, three long, two short. Pippa listened, her head on one side. "Got to go. Look—see you here tomorrow morning. Seven o'clock, say. Okay?"

"Okay. Fine," said Kate, with a momentary stab of guilt about Jon, whom she'd arranged to meet before school each morning. But maybe she and Pippa wouldn't run every day.

"I guess we should wear shorts or something," said Pippa reluctantly. "And maybe running shoes? But I've only got regular sneakers."

"I've got running shoes," said Kate, "but I'm not sure they're really good enough for running. I wouldn't know what to look for if I were going to buy real ones."

"Neither would I," said Pippa. "Hey, listen, how about a book? I could get one from the library, maybe. I live pretty near it."

"Okay," said Kate, thinking that Pippa must live near her, then, for the Kincaids' house was right across the common from the library. She was about to ask when the horn blew again and Pippa, turning away, said, "My master's voice. See you." Halfway to the lot she called back, "Got a locker mate?"

"No," Kate shouted.

"You do now!"

Kate waved her agreement, and turned to watch the Pencil round the track again. Who knows, she thought, someday I might even beat you. She watched more carefully, trying to study arm movements, leg and foot movements, trying to see how the runner controlled her breathing, trying to gauge from her face how much it really did hurt. Kate was so intent on her observations she didn't hear anyone come up behind her till she felt a hand grip her arm.

"Rab!" she exclaimed, wheeling to look up past a leather motorcycle jacket into the thin, almost grown-up face of "Rabbit" Clemson. He must, she realized, be a senior now, for he'd been a grade ahead of her in elementary school. She shook her arm free, curious, but not pleased at meeting him again. "I *am* right, aren't I? You're Rab Clemson?" The younger Rab had been a small, sullen boy who had tried, usually without success, to buy the friends he couldn't make any other way, and then often turned on them when they didn't accept. A school Christmas party came back to Kate, for first through third grades, at which Rab had interrupted a game of catch she and Jon had been playing, offering them his ball if they'd let him join them. When they'd refused, saying it was a two-person game, he'd snatched Kate's ball away. By sixth grade, Rab had become a bully, and despite her mother's commenting sympathetically on his "hungry, unloved look," Kate had never been able to forgive him.

Now he looked more brash than sullen, though still "hungry"—a spare, swaggering figure whose light brown hair stuck out in a flat awning over his eyes.

"You're right—I'm Rab," he said, flashing her a wide smile.

Where did he learn that, she wondered, for he'd rarely smiled when they'd been children. Then she saw his eyes and realized he hadn't learned after all. It was a non-smile, turned-up mouth notwithstanding.

"Well," she said uncertainly, not sure why he wasn't

saying anything more, since it looked as if he'd sought her out. "How are you?"

"I'm just fine, Bossy Kate," he said; this time she cringed at the nickname. Rab's nonsmile faded. She'd forgotten how hard and expressionless his eyes were, hungry look or no. "But you may not be fine," he went on, "if you're not careful. Hasn't anyone warned you?"

"Warned me?" she asked stupidly, trying to think what he reminded her of now. A snake, maybe; some kind of poisonous lizard . . .

"I'm surprised that Jon didn't," he said coldly, "but then, Jon's usually got his head in the clouds. Still, he of all people should have warned you about—fraternizing, I guess you could call it. Not a good idea, Kate. Dangerous. It complicates things." He tapped her arm with two fingers. "Looks bad, too, for our side." He smiled again, still only with his mouth, but this time Kate had the distinct feeling he was enjoying confusing her.

She was hurt without knowing what to be hurt about. "What do you mean?" she asked.

"Fraternizing," he repeated. "With Hastings Bay kids."

Kate shook her head. "I still don't know what you're talking about, Rab. I don't know any Hastings Bay kids, and even if I did, I don't see why . . ."

"That kid you were just talking to, that Pippa Brown. She's from Hastings Bay. And her brother, Nick; he's in my class. Let's just say there are plenty of River View kids who'd give a lot for a chance to pulverize him."

"Well, I don't know Pippa's brother," said Kate belligerently. "And frankly, I don't care what other River View kids think of him. And I certainly don't expect to be told who to talk to and who not to talk to. So forget the warning, Rab. Just forget it."

Her eyes filling with angry tears she knew she couldn't let him see, Kate ran away from the track and to her bike, and home.

4

"WHEN YOUR FEET come down," said Pippa, sprawled in the damp grass near the track the next morning, "they can come down with as much as four times your body weight." She looked at her feet in awe. "That's more than five hundred pounds. Holy smoke! Hey, feet, I didn't know you had it in you."

"Maybe they don't," said Kate, who had decided not to mention her encounter with Rab. She thumbed through another of the books Pippa had brought. *Fun Running*, it was called, and its title page proclaimed it was "The low-key book for low-key runners who don't want to make a career of their favorite sport." But even the low-key book seemed pretty high-powered: buy the right shoes (for forty or more dollars); eat the right food (no fat, almost no sugar); *think* running . . .

"Yeah, I know," said Pippa, looking over Kate's shoulder. "Sure seems like mighty serious fun, doesn't it?" She stood up. "Tell you what. Let's chuck the books, Kate. Let's just have a good time. A little low-key fun-running. Only our way, not theirs. Come on! Race you to the . . ." She looked along the unmarked track. "Well, race you to back here, okay? To where our stuff is." Pippa walked onto the track and bent over, her plump body awkwardly approximating a sprinter's starting position. "What is it they say? Must be about the same thing little kids say, no? Ready—on your mark—or is it marks? —whatever they are. Come on, slowpoke!"

Quickly, before she could become self-conscious, Kate scrambled to her feet and joined Pippa in the middle of one of the two long straight stretches.

"Get set," Pippa said, pushing Kate down to a half-kneel. "Ka-bam! That's the gun. Don't they always have a gun? GO!"

Pippa wobbled as she straightened up; probably, Kate thought, because she had to stay in the crouch waiting for me. But Kate had a feeling of power and exhilaration as her body snapped forward and her feet started moving. It was as if her body began to run before her mind could become critical and tense. Besides, she realized, finding she could easily keep up with Pippa, who glanced around at her with a determined look, there's no one here to watch but Pippa, and she's probably too busy thinking about her own running to bother about what I look like. And I'm not bouncing all over the place after all.

Soon Kate was letting her mind stretch and float with her body, and before she knew it, she was back at their starting place again, winded but not unpleasantly so, waiting for Pippa, who was several yards behind.

"Hey," Pippa panted, her face red and shiny, her curly hair dark with sweat, "that wasn't so bad. Congratulations!" She held out her hand, and when Kate had shaken it, she tumbled onto the ground next to their pile of books. "Now let's see how we should've done it."

Kate wanted to go on running, but instead she flopped down next to Pippa. For the next few minutes they pored over the books. "Yuck," said Pippa finally, holding one open to a chapter called "Runner's Blues: Injuries and Pain." She made a face, saying, "Look. Shin splints, black toe, tendonitis—are we sure we want to do this?" She flipped pages. "And," she went on, sounding even more discouraged, "it says here that you have to run —what is it?—four or five miles to work off a normal breakfast."

"But," Kate pointed out, skimming the paragraph Pippa was looking at, "it also says spaghetti's good for you. Come on." She pulled Pippa to her feet. "Let's try that running and walking thing this one suggests." She picked up another of the books. "Walk for three minutes, run for one—something like that. It's supposed to build endurance, for beginners. Here, I'll look it up."

"It's ten past eight," said Pippa. "Maybe we'd better just run." She pointed to the far end of the field and Kate saw two figures in shorts—early members of first-period gym class?—heading toward them.

"Right," Kate said, fighting self-consciousness again, and stepped onto the track. "Only I'm going to try that thing in the book."

"Okay," said Pippa, and followed, one eye on her watch.

By the time they'd gone twice around the track, alternating running and walking, the two figures had reached it and were standing there watching. One of them, Kate saw with mixed relief and embarrassment, was Becky James, the small athletic girl from her class—but the other was the Pencil.

"Do you mind?" the Pencil said, stepping into their

path as Pippa and Kate walked rapidly by. "We've got a race to train for. You can go hiking or whatever it is you're doing just about anywhere else."

"Karen," said Becky softly, "take it easy." She turned to Kate. "Karen's real serious about running," she explained apologetically. "Like she said, she's training for a race."

"It's okay," Kate said stiffly. "We were leaving anyway."

"We're training, too," Pippa said proudly. "Only we're training just to learn how to run." She smiled ingenuously. "Okay if we stick around and watch?"

Karen looked Pippa up and down. "Aren't you Nick Brown's sister?" she asked coldly.

"Well, yes," said Pippa, suddenly seeming uncomfortable. "I am, but . . ."

"I can't stop you from watching, but no, maybe it's not okay."

Kate looked at Becky, seeking an explanation, but Becky just shook her head, as if to say she could do nothing.

"Too bad," said Pippa evenly. "I'd have liked to stay. I really do think you're a good runner. Come on, Katy."

Kate turned to go, but Becky put her hand out as if to stop her, and then Karen asked, "You new around here?"

"No," said Kate, feeling her dislike growing rapidly, "not really. I've just been away for a few years."

"View or Bay?"

Kate was still trying to think of a cutting reply when Becky said quickly, "She's a Viewie, Karen; remember, she's the kid that came back? She's okay. I used to know her, from before you moved here, you know? She's a good kid. She was even class president in sixth grade, and she . . ."

Before Becky finished her sentence, Karen, completely ignoring Pippa, turned to Kate, saying, "Hi. I'm Karen Anderson. Stick around if you want. Maybe I could give you a few pointers. You didn't look too bad out there, for a beginner. Slow down, though, that's the main thing, till you've had more practice. That is, if you're going for distance. Most people do, these days."

Kate barely managed to answer, "No thanks. My friend and I have a class first period."

"Friend, huh?" Karen unzipped her jacket and stooped to tighten one shoelace. "I see. Come on, Beck." And she moved a few paces closer to the track and started doing stretching exercises.

"Bitch," said Pippa as she and Kate walked away.

"What *is* all this?" asked Kate. "What's going on?"

"You really are new, aren't you?" said Pippa. "But I thought you lived here before . . ."

"I did, but I left after sixth grade. Now come on, tell me what's going on. And don't tell me you don't get involved. That's what Jon said."

"Jon," said Pippa dreamily. "He's cute. Kind of —cuddly, even though he's so skinny. And he sure likes you."

"We've known each other forever," Kate said impatiently. "Pippa . . ."

"You know he hasn't gone out with a girl the whole time we've been in high school? At least not that I've ever seen. Not that I really know." Pippa cocked her head. "Waiting for you, I guess."

Kate was surprised, even though that was more or less what Becky had implied yesterday. "Really?" She laughed. "Well, I haven't gone out much myself . . ."

"Aha!" said Pippa.

". . . but I didn't think I was waiting for Jon. Just waiting."

"I know what you mean," said Pippa.

They had reached the steps now, and students were going inside in twos and threes. Not many, Kate noticed, were alone. Then Jon approached, by himself, from across the parking lot.

"The guy I go with," Pippa continued, "Vinnie Morano, the one who blew the horn? He graduated last year, along with a couple of other okay guys. I don't know, there aren't too many juniors or seniors who are all that great. Except," she said, dropping her voice conspiratorially, "Jon. I'd wait for him, all right, if it weren't for Vinnie. Lucky girl. See you later!" And she darted inside, as if discreetly leaving Kate and Jon alone.

Jon had seemed startled the night before when he'd come over to say hello to the rest of the Kincaids and Kate had told him she'd be going to school early to run with Pippa. She still wondered how he felt about it, but he didn't seem at all upset now. "Hi," he said cheerfully as he came up to her, shifting his books from one hip to the other. "How was your run?"

"Okay," said Kate, "till Becky and some creep named Karen—the one Pippa and I called the Pencil yesterday —came along and spoiled it."

"Karen Anderson. Right. She can be pretty sour. Of course if you really want to run, she's a good person to know."

"Yeah," said Kate drily, "but the way she treated Pippa made me not want to know her."

"Katy," said Jon, putting his arm through hers and leading her away from the steps, even though it was almost time for the first bell and Kate was still in shorts, "a lot of River View kids treat Pippa the same as Karen did. More or less, anyway."

"But *why?* She seems like a perfectly okay kid."

"She is a perfectly okay kid," Jon said sadly. "But for one thing, she's from Hastings Bay, which means that a lot of the jerkier kids won't even say hello to her, let alone get to know her enough to see that she's okay. And for another thing, more important, she's got a boyfriend and a brother who a lot of kids—well, they respect them, it's hard not to—but I guess you could say they don't like them much."

"Vinnie Morano," said Kate. "He's the boyfriend, right?"

"Right. And Nick Brown's her brother."

"I know," said Kate. "Karen made that very plain. Rab mentioned him, too," she added.

"You remember I told you Gilda was killed in a car accident last spring?"

Kate nodded, trying to ignore the sick feeling that had just begun in her stomach.

"Well, Nick was driving the other car."

"Look," said Jon later, when he and Kate had taken their lunches out to a corner of the side field, "it wasn't Nick's fault, at least the way I heard it, it wasn't. The driver of the other car, the one Gilda was in, was some college kid, and he was drunk. He went charging through an intersection without looking, and Nick's car smashed into the passenger side, into Gilda. She was killed right away."

Kate shuddered and wrapped up the rest of her egg sandwich, putting it back in its bag. "Is that why River View kids won't speak to Hastings Bay kids?"

"Partly. Everyone liked Gilda, even Rab. He'd gone out with her a couple of times. But it goes back way before that. Don't you remember kids—parents, too—talking about it when we were in elementary school, saying Hastings kids were bad? Don't you remember how every time anything happened around here—vandalism or a car wreck or a housebreak, anything like that—everyone always blamed Hastings Bay kids? Remember at the end of sixth grade, when a bunch of high school kids on motorcycles tore up part of the conservation land next to the Ice Cream Shack? Everyone said that was Hastings Bay kids, too, till the police found out it wasn't."

Kate nodded. She did remember, though she hadn't thought about it in years. But it had always seemed to her to be talk, nothing more; people looking for scapegoats, trying to get out of taking the blame themselves. "When we were little," said Jon, "I think we all just thought of Hastings Bay as the town across the river where most people's fathers didn't commute to Boston the way most of our fathers did. But it's deeper than that. When you get up to the regional school, you find out that the Hastings kids think River View is a town full of rich snobs. And that River View kids think Hastings kids are —sort of low, I guess. Low class. There was a lot of stuff last spring, even before Gilda was killed. Our old ele-

mentary school was broken into last—oh, maybe April
—and not long after that, my mom had to take a cab
home from Hastings Bay because her car broke down
there, and the driver told her this whole thing about his
brother's car being torched. He said it was kids from
View and that his brother's friends were going to cross
the bridge that night and torch a View car in retaliation.
Mom thought he was kidding, but that night a View car
was torched."

Jon stood and pulled Kate up, too; they walked to the
far end of the field where the river licked its edge. "I
think it's always been like this," he said, "at least my dad
says he remembers it from when he was a kid, only he
thinks it's getting worse. I don't know, it's like some kind
of holy war, going so far back people just concentrate on
their differences and clash with each other without
thinking much about why. Who knows what the first
thing was or who did it? I don't suppose it matters anymore, really." He picked up a stone and skimmed it into
the river; it skipped four times before it sank. "You see
why I don't get involved, the way people like Rab do, and
Pippa's brother, Nick. They hate each other's guts, those
two, and I bet they wouldn't if they both lived in the
same town. Rab hates just about everyone, anyway," he
said grimly, "even most of the kids who look up to him,
so I guess living in the same town wouldn't make much
of a difference to him. But it would to almost everyone
else, I think."

"Is it really possible," Kate asked numbly, "to stay
uninvolved?"

"I've managed since sophomore year," Jon said. "But
I don't have a whole lot of friends."

"Pippa says you're cute," Kate said, poking him, trying to cheer him up. "And cuddly."

"Cuddly!"

"Cuddly. Even though you're thin, I think she added."

"Come to me," Jon said, deepening his voice and holding out his arms. "Come to me and be cuddled."

Kate hugged him, and then they wrestled on the riverbank till the next bell, like sixth graders again, only Kate was very conscious through it all that they weren't.

5

"HERE'S SOMETHING in the paper," Dad said Saturday morning at breakfast, scanning it. "The little local one, I mean, not the *Globe.*"

"Ummm?" said Mom, handing out cantaloupe. "Now eat it, Katy; don't make such a vile face. The season won't last much longer."

Kate resisted the impulse to say "thank goodness," and winked back at Dan, who if anything hated cantaloupe worse than she.

"What gem have you found, Dad?" asked Dan, taking a deep breath in Kate's direction and holding it as he spooned in his first mouthful.

"I always think the police blotter's the most interesting thing in a small-town paper," said their father gleefully, digging at his melon, "and this certainly bears that out. The style alone—I quote:

"Tues. Sept. 4—A car driving erratically was stopped on River Road by Officer Hendricks at approximately 3:02 A.M. . . ."

Dan made frantic choking noises; Kate, playing along, pounded him. "*Approximately* 3:02, my foot," he sputtered.

"Well," said Kate solemnly, "could have been 3:02 and a half."

"Doesn't anyone care what happened at approximately 3:02?" their father asked, and their mother, with a warning glance at them both, said, "We all do, Jim. What happened at approximately 3:02?"

Dad cleared his throat and began again to read.

"Upon asking for his license and registration, the driver leaped out, leading to a black eye on the part of Officer Hendricks due to the top outside corner of the door."

"Oh, spare us," moaned Dan.

"Intrepid arrests," said Dad sternly, "are more desirable in a police department than deathless prose. Anyway . . ."

"You mean there's more?" Dan asked.

"Oh, yes:

". . . top outside corner of the door. Upon investigation, Officer Hendricks . . ."

"Who by now is operating at half visual efficiency," Dan interrupted, "his . . ."

"Or her," put in Mom.

"Or her eye slowly closing to a closed position," finished Dan. "Sorry, Dad."

"Officer Hendricks [their father went on] apprehended that [sic, he said wryly] there were in the car seven other persons, all juveniles. The driver, a juvenile domiciled in Hastings Bay, was taken to the station upon the officer noting a strong odor of alcohol and there being a case of partly opened beer in the car and later released to his parents."

Dan blinked. "No point in asking you to read that last sentence again, I suppose, is there?"

"I don't think I could," Dad answered, chuckling.

"Were the other kids from Hastings Bay, too?" Kate asked, not joining in the laughter.

"Doesn't say, dear."

"I think you should offer yourself to the police chief as a sort of station-house editor," said Mom, wiping her eyes. "I wonder if it's the same one—Laury, his name was, I think—something like that. I remember he used to drive Elizabeth Briggs crazy because he wouldn't let her change a word. Salt of the earth, of course, but no writer."

Elizabeth Briggs, Kate knew, had been the editor of the paper, and a friend of their mother's, at least until they'd moved away.

"Hey, here's something else," said Dad, frowning as he bit into his toast. "Listen to this: 'A community meeting will be held Sunday, September eleventh, at the house of Mr. and Mrs. George Dexter of Middle Lane, to discuss the state's latest nuclear waste disposal site plans.' "

"*Nuclear* waste?" asked Dan, raising his eyebrows.

"That's what it says. Maybe we should go, Julie."

"Well—if you want," Mom answered dubiously. "But you know how much shouting there always is at those things. And besides, it said the state's plans. Probably just some civic-minded citizens speaking out, that's all."

"Maybe." Dad put down his toast. "But didn't Elizabeth have a policy that nothing could go into the paper that didn't directly pertain to the town?"

"Yes, but . . ."

Dad flipped some pages over and studied the masthead. "She's still editor. I think I'll just give her a call and find out what's what."

46

"Oh, dear," Mom said, sighing, when Dad left the room. "I'm not at all sure it would be good for him to get all steamed up about something political right now."

"Just what *is* a nuclear waste disposal plant?" asked Kate.

"The leavings from things like nuclear power plants, I suppose," Mom said vaguely. "Everything industrial creates waste. I guess nuclear industry's no different."

"What's left over after bombs are made, too," said Dan thoughtfully, getting up and pushing his chair back under the table. "And medical leftovers, stuff from X-rays. Radioactive garbage." He stopped, kissing Mom. "That's what nuclear waste is. Not very pretty. Still, they probably know what they're doing. And it does have to go somewhere, after all." He twitched his jacket off the back of his chair. "Well, Family, wish me luck. I'm off to Cambridge to reacquaint myself with Harvard Square. I think I'll look up my old buddy Frank Jeffries. Maybe I'll be able to talk him into hiking up Mount Monadnock or Wachuset or something before I have to get down to business. Last fling and all. 'Bye, Kate. Don't take anything I wouldn't take."

"You either," Kate said absently, reacting only mechanically to one of the oldest of their private jokes, left over from the days when Dan had just reached his teens and their parents began making painfully tactful statements about drugs.

Dan saluted her, and left.

Their father's face, when he came back into the kitchen, was grave. "They were short of space," he said, his voice tight, "so they had to kill part of the article at the last minute. Elizabeth—who says hi, Julie, by the way, and asks you to stop in any time—Elizabeth said they figured everyone in town knew about it anyway so the background could go." He sat heavily down in his chair. "It *is* a nuclear waste disposal plant and it is indeed of local interest. One of the proposed sites is right here in River View."

Their mother looked at him blankly. "But where? There's no place. I mean . . ."

"Upstream," he said. "Off River Road. It seems there's some old town land there, never built on or used. And there are no houses for miles on the upstream side of it. The state wants to take it by eminent domain if the town won't sell, or maybe anyway, to clear the title. There's a special town meeting about it in a while, six weeks, she said. I think I'll stroll over to River Road this morning and take a look. Anyone want to come?"

"I should finish the unpacking," said Mom doubtfully. "There's still some guest-room stuff. But maybe—there's no danger, Jim, though, is there? I mean Dan said . . ."

"Dan," said their father, "is a very smart young man and a very well-informed one. But as far as I know no one really understands the dangers connected with disposing of nuclear waste. I think they usually put it in containers, but no one's been doing that for long enough to have more than a few nasty theories about what happens if the containers leak. As most of them are bound to do sooner or later." He pushed his chair back and stood up. "I've been looking for something to sink my teeth into," he said. "I hadn't planned on anything quite this explosive—forgive the pun—but . . ." He rubbed his hands together. "I'm sure a little historical perspective wouldn't hurt, added to all the scientific expertise everyone'll probably trot out."

In the end, they all three went to River Road, and Jon, whom they ran into on the way, went along with them, pushing his bike. "I don't know much about it, Mr. Kincaid," he said as they walked briskly down Route 40. "But my folks were all steamed up about it when it was first proposed. My dad said anyone who wants to dispose of anything near a river ought to have his head examined."

"I'm inclined to agree," said Kate's father. "Maybe I'll give him a call. Is he going to the meeting Saturday?"

"I don't know," said Jon. "Probably."

As they reached the bridge, Jon stopped and touched Kate's shoulder, pointing up with his other hand. "Look!"

A red-winged blackbird, Kate's favorite, was flying low over the river, heading downstream.

"Pretty creature," said Dad, as they all watched the bird. "Not too many of those in Providence."

Kate squeezed her father's hand and then, as they turned onto River Road, she fell back behind her parents, walking with Jon.

"Your dad sets quite a pace, Miss Kettle."

"Doctor's orders, Mr. Pot, doctor's orders."

"How is he?"

"Okay as far as I know. I think Mom's worried about him getting too excited about this waste thing, though."

"I'm not surprised," Jon said. "It was the A-number-one topic with my folks and their friends for weeks awhile ago. I think my folks are getting a little sick of it now, but I didn't want to say that to your dad. Besides, maybe he could stir them up again, if he's up to it, of course. Someone should."

"What do you mean?"

"As I said, I don't know a lot about it, but I do know it isn't waste from electrical plants they're talking about, or even from hospitals. It's waste from weapons. The radioactive stuff from bombs and missiles, the ones they don't trust anymore because they're too old, and the ones they've made mistakes on. Seems they want to experiment with how to dispose of that stuff in the 'crowded Northeast,' as they call it, because they figure they'll run out of space out West in the desert pretty soon. 'Preparedness is all,' I think one article said. Of course, as my dad pointed out, what it also means is that they'll have to truck weapons or parts of weapons through the streets of the 'crowded Northeast' to get them to the plant to be destroyed. One mistake, one ordinary traffic accident —well, you don't want any mistakes at all with those babies."

Kate stopped, trying to take it in. The sun was shining; the river was flowing serenely to their right; smoke was rising lazily from a farmhouse on their left; and she and Jon and her parents had just seen, with great pleasure, a red-winged blackbird. "I can't—you really mean *bombs?*"

Jon nodded.

"But . . ."

"I know, Katy," he said sympathetically. " 'To everything there is a season,' " he quoted softly. " 'A time to be born and a time to die. A time to kill . . .' But the thing is, I'm not sure there's ever a time for that. I mean, who is anyone trying to kid? The reason you make a weapon is to kill people. People. People like you and me, babies, old ladies, dogs. And when you have to throw that weapon away . . ."

"Don't, Jon," Kate said, her hands going involuntarily to her ears. "Don't."

"Miss Kettle," he said, still more softly. "Even if you don't choose to listen or to see, it's going to happen."

The proposed site was nothing but a huge field, sloping down to the water. Goldenrod nodded in it; runaway blackberry bushes thickened it. Cattails grew along the river and birds sang at the edge of the woods.

"Right about here, Mr. Kincaid," Jon said, standing in the middle of the field and holding his arms out like a scarecrow. "My dad said something about underground tanks, lined with lead to keep the radiation in. They'd go almost as far as the river from right about here, he said."

"But the river overflows in the spring," said Kate's father, frowning.

"Right. And runs so fast in the spring that it undercuts its banks a little more each year. But lead, the prophets say, rusteth not, neither does it leak."

How could I have thought, Kate admonished herself, watching Jon, that he hasn't grown up? He's grown up more than I; no wonder he still wants to go fishing and frogging while he can and play Miss Kettle and Mr. Pot and not get involved in whatever stupid feud is going on between River View and Hastings Bay. Love for him flooded her; not, she thought, the kind of love Pippa had talked about, but a quiet, permanent bond with a depth she hadn't thought possible.

Her mother was standing a little apart from the rest

of them, her face white, looking beyond the goldenrod and cattails to the river. Instinctively Kate went to her and put an arm around her. "And you a pacifist," she said softly, seeing without surprise that her mother was close to tears.

Mrs. Kincaid embraced her daughter wordlessly, and then all four of them turned and walked back up River Road in silence.

6

"THE WINGS of spiders . . ." Jon said absently, toying with his illegal beer.

"The *what?*" Kate moved closer to Jon; they were parked in his father's car, on River Road a mile or so north of the site. She'd had two beers herself, which was more than enough, she knew, to make her lightheaded. "Spiders don't have wings, dopey."

"No," said Jon, stretching against the driver's seat. "But they ought to. Look at their webs, masterpieces of intricacy, flawlessly engineered . . ."

"For *catching* flies, not for fly*ing*," Kate said, kissing him on the end of his nose without thinking and then sitting back, surprised at herself. She didn't remember ever kissing him before.

"Well," he said, rubbing his nose gently, not looking at her. "Well."

"Let's get out and walk," Kate said, actually wanting to run and partly wishing it were tomorrow and she were running with Pippa, relaxed and easy.

"Suits me," said Jon, opening his door. "I don't much go for steering wheels in the chest anyway." It didn't look as if he was going to say anything more about the kiss.

But he did take her hand now and then as they walked.

"Remember," said Jon, "when we tried to sail that old boat?"

"Oh, good grief, yes!" It had been someone's abandoned and very leaky rowboat, a beamy punt, with, as Jon had put it, two sterns. They'd strung a bedspread between two oars and set off across the river in a stiff west wind, each holding an oar. They'd made it across to the Hastings Bay side, but of course couldn't go back against the wind.

"What did we call her?" Kate asked.

"The *Flying Balloon*," Jon answered promptly. "Remember: 'I'll see you soon, in the *Flying Balloon*.'"

"Oh—yes! 'By the light of the moon, in the *Flying Balloon*, we'll sail and we'll croon, this livelong June.' Oh, brother. Tell me I didn't write that. Tell me we were only about seven and didn't know any better."

"You didn't write it, we both did. We were ten. We probably did know better."

"The *Flying Balloon*," Kate said softly.

"Remember the igloo?" asked Jon, sitting down on the bank and pulling her down beside him.

"No—yes! We tried to cut the snow in blocks but it was too crumbly."

"Right." He plucked a piece of grass and put it in his mouth. "So we ended up making a sort of hill and trying to hollow it out."

"It worked—didn't it?"

"Until your brother came along and stomped on it."

"I'd forgotten; you're right. That's maybe the one rotten thing Dan ever did."

"That and be—I don't know, not stuffy, but—well, *right*."

54

"Ummm," she said. "Dutiful, maybe. Honorable, like in Shakespeare." She glanced over at Jon. The moon shone on his face, making the hollows under his cheekbones dark and mysterious; his hair glowed. "Dan signed up for the draft," she said, "the day we got here."

"I figured he would."

"Will you? I mean, would you if you were eighteen?"

"No," he said, more to himself than to her, she thought. "No. I wouldn't and I won't."

"Would you go to jail if there was a war or something and they actually called people up?"

"You know I would. So would you. Wouldn't you?"

"I—I think so." But she knew she might give in at the last minute. Just the idea of jail had always given her claustrophobia.

Jon stood up. "Well," he said, "we won't need to worry, will we? Any war bad enough to reactivate the draft probably won't give anyone time to report for duty. We'll all be cooked before we can even think about what's happening. Fast, sort of like in my mom's microwave."

Kate stood, too, facing him; he was smiling but his eyes were leaden, as if they'd seen something she hadn't. "That won't happen," she said stubbornly.

Instead of answering, Jon opened the can of beer he'd brought with him, and offered it to her as they walked.

It felt good walking with him at night, past places they'd known as children but had never been to together after dark, past places she'd forgotten. It felt good, too, watching the moonlight play in his hair, watching his face when he wasn't aware she was looking at him. Am I in love with him? she wondered, startled at the idea, put in her mind, she supposed, by Pippa. In love as opposed to loving. I could pretend to be, I know that. But am I really?

"A penny," Jon said.

Kate shook her head.

"The rule," he admonished her. They'd made a rule in fourth grade, when one of them had found the phrase "A penny for your thoughts" in a book. You had to pay up if you didn't answer, instead of paying if you got an answer.

"You owe me a dime, then," he said, adding "inflation" when she protested.

They approached Route 40 and the bridge that linked River View to Hastings Bay. Jon stopped in the brush beside the bottom-scraped bank, pointing to where a bonfire winked across at them. "See?" he said. "They do that every night. Every weekend night, anyway, and some weeknights."

"It's not a bad idea," Kate said, as she had before. "Why don't we do it, too? You and me, I mean."

"I told you the River View police got nervous when someone did. There's no law or anything against it, but if anyone lit a fire here, the police would come."

"Let's light one anyway," said Kate, bending over to gather twigs. "Just a little, careful one."

"We've been drinking, Katy. That's what they look for."

"We're not drunk."

"No. But we're minors."

"Mr. Goody-goody," she said, angry. "Now who's stuffy?"

He shrugged.

"Well, maybe I'll go across to their fire, then, and say hello." She started onto the bridge, but felt his hand gripping her arm.

"No, Katy," he said. "They wouldn't want you."

She tried to pull away. "Don't be ridiculous. They don't know me. They don't even know I'm from River View, if you're worried about that silly whatever-you-call-it—feud. Only Pippa knows."

"Just about every kid in school knows, stupid. You've been there four days. You think no one's noticed?"

"But, Jon, it's crazy," she said, really mad now. "It's crazy. I like Pippa; maybe there are others I'd like. I'm not part of their feud, and what's more I'm not going to be forced into being part of it."

She broke free of him and ran.

She was sure he'd stop her, but he just stood at the edge of the bridge, watching. Coward, she thought, and went on running, the wind in her face, her feet feeling light and winged, making her picture Mercury in her sixth-grade mythology book. At first she was so caught up in her own motion that she wasn't conscious of the raucousness of the voices from the bonfire, but when she got almost across the bridge, she heard them more clearly and she slowed to a jog, then to a walk. It didn't sound as much like a party as she'd thought, and it was just boys' voices that she heard. Stealthily, she crept closer.

Five or six boys were sitting around the fire, smoking. The only one she recognized was Skid Johnson, the boy who'd peeled into the parking lot the first day of school; the firelight was full on him.

She could catch only snatches of sentences:

"God damn Viewie creeps . . ." Skid was snarling.

". . . it's their stinking attitude that gets me . . ."

"Yeah, like just *being* there means . . . done something." That was Skid again.

"So what did he say, Skid?"

"He said . . ." Kate could see Skid move to crouch by the fire, a little away from the others, facing them, firelight dancing on his powerful face. ". . . one more time . . . haul me in, even if he had to make up a charge."

"Which," said another boy loudly, above the laughter that followed, "shouldn't be too hard, Skid, seeing as how you and minor transporting are kind of good friends."

"Yeah, well, Nick said . . ."

Pippa's brother again, thought Kate as the voices dropped and the boys drew closer together.

She couldn't hear what he was supposed to have said.

"Kate? Katy?" came a whisper behind her, and then Jon's hand was on her arm, lightly this time. "Come on, let's go."

More grateful than mad now, she turned willingly and let him lead her back to the bridge.

"I'm sorry," he said when they got back. "But I don't think they'd understand you were there just to make friends."

Kate realized she agreed now. "No. No, you're right. I don't think they would either." She took the beer can he held out to her. "But there's got to be a way."

"Maybe you're on to one—a slow one, but the best one there is."

"What's that?" She handed him back the can.

"You and Pippa. That's what it takes," he said. "Kids from both sides being friends. If there were more Kates and Pippas, the whole thing might go away. You were lucky, though, meeting her before you knew."

"Pippa must have known."

"Yes, but she didn't know where you were from till it was too late. And besides, no one would mess with Pippa, no one from either side."

"Why not?"

"Because of Nick. Her boyfriend, too, a little. But mostly Nick."

"All I hear is Nick, Nick, Nick."

"Skid's the loudest, but if the Hastings kids have a real leader, it's Nick."

"So anyone who wanted to change things would have to change him," said Kate slowly.

"Him, and Rab on our side. Rab's worse. Katy . . ."

She shook her head; she was a little dizzy from the beer. "It's a dumb feud and as you said, I haven't been warned—brainwashed—like the others. And they don't know me. So—so maybe I ought to be the one to try to change it. Like you said, more Kates and Pippas . . ."

"I almost believe you *could* change it if anyone could."

"But you still don't think it can be done, right?"

His eyes looked into hers, then away, and whatever was troubling him seemed to surface briefly and then recede.

"Right?" she asked more softly.

"Freshman year," he told her, "I tried it. I tried not to listen to the brainwashing. I made friends with a Hastings kid, just like you with Pippa. Hank—he was in the band, and he liked model ships and folk music and being outside—a lot of the things I like. He didn't want to be part of the feud any more than I did. We started hanging around together. Then one night Rab and his pals got hold of me, and Nick got hold of Hank."

"And?"

Abruptly, Jon turned around and pulled up his shirt. On one side of his spine was a thin T-shaped scar, puckered at the edges.

"The shape's no accident," he said, tucking his shirt back in and facing her again. "T stands for traitor. That's what Rab said as he branded me: T for traitor."

"Oh, my God!" Kate put her arms around him, a sob catching in her throat. "Oh, Jon! I can't believe even Rab would do that, not to anyone! Your poor back."

"Rab's like that, Katy," Jon said into her hair. "He's gotten much worse than he was when we were in sixth grade. But some kids do look up to him now, like he's some kind of king. Following him is better to them, I guess, than being his victims. He uses the feud to get people on his side, to make people think he's tough. He's done that since about a year after you left, when a bunch of kids from Hastings beat up his little brother. And he's . . ." Jon paused for a moment. "Anyway, it wasn't a very deep burn, and it was quick. It stopped hurting, on the outside anyway, a long time ago. Maybe it's cowardly, but it just didn't seem worth it after that to be part of their crazy game." He pushed away from her and held her at arm's length. "You do what you want to do; I can't stop you. Maybe you and Pippa will have better luck, being girls. Hey . . ." He touched her cheek. "Hey, no tears. It's an old hurt. Come on," he said, taking her hand. "Come see my models. We both need cheering up."

. . .

They drove very carefully, because of the beer, to Jon's house and, suppressing laughter, crept across the front porch—"Careful, that board squeaks, step here"—into the house, and up—avoiding the fourth stair, which also squeaked—to Jon's room.

"They look better in moonlight anyway," Jon whispered, pointing to a table under his wide window.

I haven't been in this room, Kate realized, since I was twelve, and it's just the same. She turned, smiling that thought to him, and he, clearly understanding, smiled back.

"This one's the best," he whispered, holding up a clipper ship model. "The *Flying Cloud*. Better than the old *Balloon*, isn't she?"

Kate nodded; the rigging dripped silver in the moonlight, intricate and lacy. "Spider's wings," she whispered, and he said, "Yes."

She examined the ships, one by one. The *Flying Cloud* was the most beautiful and the most complex, but each of the others had something special about it: tiny varnished planks on the deck; lifeboats swinging from working davits; a smoothly carved and polished pinrail —something on each that attested to Jon's loving patience.

"They're a long way," she said, "from that catboat you did."

"My first." He reached to a bookcase behind him and handed her a simple rough model, with a crude balsawood hull and a single mast.

But even on that one the rigging was perfect.

"We'd better go back out," he whispered, "before we wake someone."

"I'd better leave," she said, glancing at her watch; it was 2 A.M.

"I'll walk you home."

He took her hand and they went through the quiet streets, shoulders touching, and she felt their four years apart slip away as if they'd never been.

7

IT WAS a golden morning, bright and crisp and cool; perfect, Kate realized when she stepped sleepily outside, for running.

She hadn't slept well, thinking in circles about Jon's brand and what had led to it. No matter what angle she approached it from, she always came back to the same thing: no one knows me here; I could do something about it—try to, anyway.

But that thought sent her back to her old nickname, Bossy Kate. Wouldn't it seem like that? Bossy and presumptuous?

To wake herself up, Kate jogged across the common, past the neat sleeping houses and out onto Route 40. Pippa was meeting her at the bridge to see how far they could run along River Road, but Kate's legs felt like stretching and she broke into a real run prematurely, trying to free herself from her troubling thoughts. Leafy branches, heavy with the rain that had fallen briefly a few hours earlier, brushed against her arms and dripped their moisture on her head and back, cooling her before she was hot. The blue sky seemed close, as if she could run uphill right into it.

She saw Pippa long before she reached her, plump

body snuggled against one of the posts that marked the beginning of the bridge, looking down at the water.

"Hi," said Kate, running up to her, trying to pretend she wasn't winded.

Pippa looked at her with obvious amusement. "Morning. How long you think you're gonna last on River Road if you start out panting like that?"

Kate flung her arms wide, awake now and close to cheerful. "Forever!" she said, and, as if saying so would clinch it, "I feel wonderful, terrific, strong as an ox!"

"Oh, yeah? Then how come your face is red and there's sweat pouring off it?"

"Illusion." Kate wiped her forehead. "Wow! What a beautiful morning."

" 'Wow, what a beautiful morning,' " Pippa sang obligingly, " 'Wow, what a beautiful day . . .' "

They finished their version of the song together at the top of their lungs, or what lungs Kate had left.

But Kate found last night's thoughts were still there after all.

"Pippa," she asked, "do you know a kid named Hank?"

Pippa looked startled. "I know two kids named Hank," she said. "Hank Morelli and Hank Holland. Which one do you mean?"

"I don't know. The one who was friends with my friend Jon until—well, if you know him, you probably know what happened."

"Until my brother told him not to be friends anymore," said Pippa slowly. "Hank Morelli."

"Jon," said Kate, "got branded with a T for that friendship. T for traitor. By Rab Clemson. He still has the scar."

"Kate, don't."

"Don't what?"

"Don't say you want to get back at Nick for that."

"I don't know," said Kate, watching Pippa's face. "I guess it was too long ago for that. But Jon says there've been other things, too, for a long time. And—Pippa, isn't that kind of terrible? Shouldn't someone try to stop it?"

"Sure," said Pippa, "but who? No one wants to, Katy, no one dares try, anyway."

"Maybe," said Kate quietly—but her heart was beating very fast—"maybe I want to." She spoke quickly, cutting Pippa off. "But first I have to know more about it. Back with that thing with Jon and Hank, what —this is kind of blunt—what did your brother do to Hank? I mean, since Rab burned Jon . . ."

"Nothing," said Pippa shortly. "Nick's not like that. He talked to him, that's all. Nick doesn't beat people up. Some of the others do, Skid Johnson, for instance. But not Nick."

Kate wondered if Skid had acted on Nick's orders, but thought better of asking. Instead she said, "Well, I think the whole thing's insane."

"Right," said Pippa, drawing the toe of one new running shoe back and forth in the dirt by the post. "Sure it's insane. Childish, too. But, Katy, you can't stop it."

"Why not? Why can't I try?" Kate felt excited now, eager. "No one really knows me; it's as if I really were new in town. Maybe I could talk to kids on both sides, be neutral, sort of."

"They wouldn't think you were neutral. And they wouldn't listen."

"You mean your brother wouldn't?" Kate asked carefully.

Pippa grinned. "Oh, he'd probably listen, or pretend to, anyway. He'll listen to anything a girl has to say to him. But he wouldn't do anything. And Rab, from your own side—he wouldn't even go that far."

"Rab used to want friends. I bet he still does, underneath."

"Katy," said Pippa quietly, "Rab's the kind of kid who used to like to pull the legs off bugs. Now he's the kind who runs over squirrels other people try to dodge. All he wants is allies, not friends."

"God," said Kate.

"Yeah." Pippa put her hand on Kate's arm. "C'mon. Let's run. You're not winded anymore, and I promised Mom I'd be home by ten-thirty to go to mass."

"It's not even eight yet," Kate persisted. "Look, could you just give me some background, maybe, about Nick? Could you just tell me about the Gilda thing? If I have to see Nick, I should know about that. Rab dated her, right?"

"Nick doesn't talk about Gilda," Pippa said, turning away. "I don't think you should mention her to him. Yes"—she turned back—"Rab went out with her once or twice. I don't think it was any big thing, though. The accident wasn't Nick's fault. The car Gilda was in went right through the intersection without looking. Nick couldn't have stopped. Nick went to see her mother; he went to the funeral. But Gilda's brothers wouldn't let him in. So he stood outside the church, and then he went to the cemetery and stood under a tree where no one could see him. He prayed for her, he told Mom. And I think he probably did. He carries Gilda around his neck, Kate, like the sailor in the poem did that dead bird. Alba —whatever it was."

"Albatross," said Kate. She touched Pippa's arm. "I'm sorry. But I'm glad you told me. It makes him less of an enemy. Don't you see? Maybe if other View kids could hear what you just said . . ."

"They'd laugh," Pippa said firmly. "And they wouldn't believe it." She turned to Kate and Kate was astonished to see that her eyes were pleading. "Kate, it won't work. It's a great idea but it won't work. The whole thing goes back too far, and there are too many kids like Skid and Rab who want to keep it going. Last summer? Late August, I think it was. Some kids from your side came across the river to ours and went to a place called The Hut for ice cream. And there was a big fight. The cops came and banged their nightsticks around and a couple of kids from both sides ended up in the hospital, only no one's sure who put them there, other kids or the cops."

"Our side, your side, both sides," said Kate in disgust. "Don't you see that's the trouble?" She waited for Pippa to respond and then, giving up for the time being, said, "Okay, let's run. Maybe it'll clear my brain."

"Now you're talking!" Pippa tapped Kate's shoulder lightly. "Hey, look, there's *some* progress. I mean, there's us, isn't there? Talking about it, being friends?" She peered at Kate. "We are friends, aren't we?"

"Looks like it," said Kate, smiling, thinking of her talk with Jon.

"That's a beginning, isn't it? Ready? Let's go!"

They sprinted off, pretending to race at first, but then

they switched to a steady jog, turning out at River Road and heading up toward the school. When they got there, Pippa, her face very red, slowed to a fast walk, and so Kate did also, saying, "Want to stop?" Pippa shook her head and after a few minutes ran again. She was slower than Kate, and she got winded faster. But Kate knew by now that she made up in spunk for what she lacked in endurance, and she was getting better all the time. Kate matched her pace to Pippa's, but a quarter mile or so beyond the school, she felt herself beginning to flag and wanted to end with one quick burst—"the flying feeling," she'd come to call it. So she said, "Pip?" and when Pippa turned, her face streaming sweat, Kate said, "I'm going to speed up a bit, then stop. Okay?"

Pippa nodded and Kate took off again, deciding to make her feet go as fast as she could. As the road blurred in front of her, she felt joy surge through her body, despite the ache in her lungs and legs that told her she'd done enough. Damn, she thought, knowing she should probably stop but not wanting to let go of the joy. A farm stand, piled with squash and beans and pumpkins, flew by; a dog started barking but then gave up and just watched; a small boy on roller skates stared. She could hardly breathe now and sweat was pouring into her eyes, so she eased off to a jog, then at last to a walk, circling a thick oak that interrupted a stone wall by the side of the road, waiting for Pippa, slowing her heart and catching her breath, her mind blissfully empty, her body tingling and the joy staying with her as the aches subsided.

"Man," Pippa panted, coming up at a slow trot, "do you look beautiful running or do you look beautiful running? I think you should go out for track. I'm sure they'd let you sign up."

"Nope," said Kate. "Don't want to. I'm having too much fun on my own." She clapped Pippa on the shoulder. "Hey, you didn't do so bad yourself, friend."

"Well, I came the whole way, at least," said Pippa. She cocked her head in the way Kate had almost come to expect. "Know what? I've lost four pounds since we started."

"Hey, that's terrific!" Kate gave her a sweaty hug, then felt how exhausted Pippa was and said, "Let's walk around a bit, okay? Nice and easy. I had a ballet teacher once who said don't ever sit down after a workout, walk around till your heart stops pounding."

"Ballet, huh?"

Kate made a face; it had been nothing. "Just at this school I went to," she said. "In Providence. They had some idea about dance making women graceful—at least less clumsy—and it was either ballet or ballroom."

"Yuck," said Pippa. "You mean real ballroom? Like the weird stuff people's parents do?"

"Grandparents," said Kate. "Waltzes, fox trots."

Pippa giggled. "Did you ever see a fox trot?"

"Or a bunny hop?" said Kate.

"Or a snake crawl?"

"Snake crawl!" said Kate. "What kind of a dance is that?"

Pippa threw herself onto the grass and wiggled forward as sinuously as her round body allowed. "I made it up," she said, scrambling to her feet. "Think it'll catch on?"

"Definitely." Kate felt a different kind of joy begin to flood her. "Pip," she said, trying to sound casual but wanting somehow to mark the moment, "you know what?"

"Probably not. What?"

"You're fun."

Pippa blushed. "So are you," she said, kicking at a stone. She turned to Kate as they walked. "Look," she said, "you want to meet my brother, it's okay with me. Maybe I can get Mom to invite you for dinner next week, okay? Say Thursday?"

"Sure," said Kate, surprised.

Pippa grinned. "Only, listen, watch out for him. He —he's this kind of macho type who thinks he's God's gift to women. I think I'd better warn him you're spoken for, okay?"

"Am I?"

"Aren't you?"

Kate smiled. "Somehow I don't think of Jon that way," she said.

"Oh, come on. He's a guy, you're a girl. Simplest thing in the world."

"Oh, yeah?" It had never seemed so to Kate.

"Maybe you're right," said Pippa, sitting down on the edge of the stone wall they'd been following back toward school; Kate sat next to her. "Maybe it's not so simple." She sighed. "It's weird, though. Vinnie's okay, but I'd give anything to go out with a guy like Jon, at least once or twice, and there you are, seeing him all the time, and not even caring."

"I do care," said Kate, "very much. But it's like he's part of me. A brother, only more than that."

"The kind of guy," said Pippa, "who any sensible girl would end up marrying."

Kate laughed. "Incest!" she said. "That's what it would be. Besides—marry? I don't want to think about that for a long time."

"You don't?" Pippa sounded surprised. "I sure do. What do you want, then?"

"Lord," said Kate. "I don't know." She leaned back, holding on to the edge of the wall with her hands, feeling her shoulders stretch as they took her weight. "What do I want? To write a great poem, maybe. To go places —everywhere—Europe, Russia, the North Pole, Africa. To meet hundreds of people, all kinds. To feel everything—joy, pain, terror, love, hate. To—to get inside the minds of everyone in the whole world." She had almost forgotten Pippa by now, and where she was. "To feel what they feel and know whatever truth it is they know."

Pippa was silent for a while. Then she said softly, "Wow, you're really something, you know that?"

Kate jumped, as if waking up. "No," she answered. "No, I'm not. Just melodramatic." But she was shaking a little inside, for she knew she'd never have said all that to Chelsea, and wasn't sure she'd have said it to Jon.

But then Jon would have known it anyway.

"What do you want, Pippa?" she asked, partly to be polite and move the focus away from herself, but also because she was curious.

Pippa laughed. "Oh, jerky things," she said. "I guess what I want most is to be happy. To have a happy life, with no troubles like my mom's always had. I want ordinary things. A husband, a nice house, a couple of kids, and a dog. No pain, no terror, like you. I want to get up and make bacon and eggs and toast and juice and coffee, a real breakfast for my family—*my* family—every morning, and see the kids off to school and my husband off to work"—she laughed again—"and then maybe go outside and run with a good friend."

"You'll need to run," said Kate, feigning sternness, "after enough of those breakfasts."

"Home in time for lunch," said Pippa cheerfully. Then she clapped her hand over her mouth, repeating, "Lunch! Oh, no. I knew I should've gone to early mass. What time is it?"

"Ten to nine," said Kate. "You've got hours." She stood up. "But I guess we should start back even so."

"Yeah, I guess," said Pippa, getting up. "Should I ask my mom about dinner?"

"Sure."

"You want to bring Jon?"

Kate thought a minute as they walked, then said, "No. It'd be better without him. But thanks." She turned to Pippa. "*You* want me to bring Jon?"

"No, of course not. He's yours, even if you don't think he is. Besides, there's Vinnie."

"Jon," said Kate, "isn't anybody's. Hey, what about Vinnie? Are you . . ."

"He likes me a lot," said Pippa, as if choosing her words carefully. "And I like him. But bells don't ring when I'm with him, you know what I mean? He works for my dad. My dad has a garage, a service station. Nick helps out there, too, sometimes. Vinnie's sort of a mechanic; he's pretty good, my dad says. You need a car fixed, you just tell me. We've been going out since just before he graduated. He's really okay—more than that. It's just that he's like most guys I've always known, and Jon isn't. But I do like him a lot." She laughed. "Except he's a slobby kisser sometimes, you know? Does Jon get like that? Man, I wish guys would learn how to kiss!"

"No," said Kate, a little enviously. "No, Jon doesn't get like that. At least not so far. I told you, it's not that kind of relationship. At least not—no, it's not that kind of relationship."

Pippa stood still, giving Kate a long look. Then she started walking again and said, "Well, Nick'll be more attentive, anyway, without Jon there. He might even like you."

"I'm not after that," Kate said. "I just want to talk to him."

"How do you know you're not after that? He's a pretty good-looking guy."

Kate shrugged.

"I know," said Pippa gently. "Your mind's on higher things. My superior friend," she said, but still gently, with fondness. "My friend the peacemaker, with all the brains."

"Doesn't it bother you?" Kate asked curiously; they had almost reached the river. "The whole mess? Kids not speaking to each other, beating each other up?"

"Yeah, it bothers me. It bothers me especially when someone gets hurt. I worry about Nick, about Vinnie, other kids. But I figure we'll all be out of here in another couple of years, and it'll die down, for us, anyway. The kids in their twenties don't get involved much. For a while, sure, when they're just out of high school, like

Vinnie's still in it, a little. But then the kids from your side go away to college, and the kids from our side get jobs, and they get too busy to bother about each other anymore."

"Is that how it really is?" Kate asked, startled. "College for River View, jobs for Hastings?"

"Yeah," said Pippa, "pretty much. Oh, there are exceptions here and there. But, yeah, that's how it is."

⅏8

KATE FOUND Jon outside, practicing his guitar in his back-yard under a gnarled pine she remembered climbing years earlier. He lifted his head, but she could see he didn't want to be interrupted. So, after listening a few minutes and thinking how good he'd gotten, she went away and walked slowly home.

At home her parents and Dan were just finishing breakfast amid a neat pile of Sunday papers. "There you are," said her mother, pouring her some juice. "Have a nice run? Bacon and eggs? French toast?"

"I'll fix it," Kate said indifferently. "You go read the paper."

Her mother lingered as the others left. "Anything wrong, pal?" she asked.

"No." Kate turned; it had always been hard to lie to her mother, to hide things from her. "At least—nothing for publication yet. Okay?"

"Okay." Her mother gave her a quick squeeze. "Just want to remind you I'm here. Same for Daddy and Dan."

Kate hugged her back. "Thank goodness for families," she said.

Her mother blew her a kiss and left.

Alone in the sunny kitchen, Kate scrambled some eggs and popped two pieces of bread into the toaster. French toast would have been nice but it seemed like too much bother.

She tried to concentrate on the eggs, on scraping the mixture into neat moist balls in the pan, tried to think only of that and keep the rest of her mind blank. But as usual, it didn't work. Why, she wondered, plopping the eggs onto a plate, is it impossible to think of nothing? Even thinking about not thinking of anything is thinking of something.

She moved yesterday's crossword puzzle away from her place (Dan must have been sitting there; he was the crossword-puzzle addict) and sat down—then jumped up again to get her now-cold toast and spread it with butter and raspberry jam. But the butter made hard lumps on the cold toast, so she pried most of it off and returned it, crumbs and all, to the dish, and had the jam alone. It didn't taste as good.

"Bossy Kate," she said aloud, thinking of how sure of herself she must have sounded to Pippa.

But branding people—branding Jon—that's going too far. And torching cars.

Jon, she told herself, eating eggs but not tasting them, doesn't really care about the feud.

No.

That's wrong.

Jon cares, but he cares so much he wants to avoid it. It hurts him, for some reason. Well. His back. Of course his back. And that someone would do that to him.

Not, she thought, chasing the last blob of egg around her plate, that he was ever part of things much anyway.

People admire Jon, though, are fond of him. But not close to him.

Except me, of course.

Are we in love?

Why do I keep wondering about that? She shook the idea away, hard.

Would it be fair to ask him to help get the two towns together?

He's a thinker, a watcher. So am I, but I'm a doer, too. Is it fair to ask a person like Jon to change?

No matter what Pippa says, she thought, taking her plate to the sink and rinsing it, there'll always be new crops of freshmen to carry on the feud. Unless it's stopped, they'll inherit it, as Jon said, like people who inherit the war in the Middle East. And like the little wide-eyed children in Nothern Ireland, with their rocks and their homemade gasoline bombs. Those kids grow up year after year into a civil war that's older than they are, and hate each other automatically because that's how it's always been.

Mom would say the feud's like that, like a war, and that it ought to be stopped.

Kate went back to the table and sat for a long time, her mind moving in jolts and circles. But no matter how many times she told herself she had no business, after four years away, to try to stop a quarrel that wasn't her own, she kept coming back to the fact that it was just *because* she'd been away that she might be the most qualified to stop it.

And that stopping it was right, even though with that realization came a terrible gnawing dread that wouldn't leave her alone.

"Sorry about this morning," said Jon as Kate met him on her porch that evening; her parents had gone to the waste-disposal meeting and Jon had called to ask if she wanted to go to the Ice Cream Shack.

"It's okay," Kate said lightly, determined not to involve him any more than she had to. "Hey—you sounded pretty good on that guitar."

"Yeah, I guess I've improved. Ice Cream Shack?"

"Sure."

"It'll seem pretty tame, probably," he said, as they went down the steps and across the common, "after Providence. Most of the kids here would give anything to live in a city."

"You?"

He gave her a look. "You know me better. But a lot of the others are bored."

That's true, she thought; there can't be much around here for kids our age to do.

They walked in silence out of the town center and along Route 40. It was a starry night, with a thin edge to the air, foretelling winter.

It looked as if about a quarter of their old elementary school class was at the Ice Cream Shack, along with a few of the newer people. Becky James and Karen Anderson were leaning against someone's car and eating cones greedily, as if they were starved. Becky waved to Kate and Jon, but Karen, Kate noticed, looked away, obviously pretending she hadn't seen them. Charlie Moss was nearby, tossing a Frisbee around with two other boys; Rab, a walking cliché in his leather jacket, was draped over a motorcycle talking to a pack of adoring younger boys. "Compensating for his own deepest lacks," said Jon easily, watching him. "As long as I keep telling myself that, I can almost control what my stomach does every time I see him."

"How does he react to you?" Kate asked curiously —but just then, Rab detached himself from the younger boys and sauntered over, heading for Kate, ignoring Jon. "That's how," Jon whispered when Rab was still out of earshot. "I don't exist. And mostly that's how I react to him, too." But as Rab approached, Jon nodded curtly to him. Then he said loudly to Kate, "Hot fudge, right?" Kate said yes, not sure whether to be amused or troubled, and Jon joined the ice cream line, standing in it sideways as if trying to keep her in sight.

"So, Kate," said Rab, jutting his chin after Jon. "You're really going with him, huh? What a waste!"

Before she could think of how to answer, Rab gave her what she imagined he thought was a dazzling smile, but again it looked like a cardboard one he'd pulled out of his pocket and pasted on. "My apologies for the other day," he said grandly, "about your friend, I mean. Pippa's not a bad kid, herself. But . . ." He put his right hand lightly on her arm. "You know—politics."

That elegant hand, she thought, moving her arm out from under it, branded a T in my best friend's back, heated a knife and held it against his bare skin. "Oh?" she said, purposely vague. "The only trouble is, Rab, I don't belong to either party. And I intend to remain independent." She went on, saccharine-sweet. "The thing that amazes me is how many otherwise intelligent people around here have suddenly stopped thinking for themselves."

Before she could lose what remained of her nerve, she walked away to join Jon, who was still standing in line.

" 'Sail on, silvergirl,' " he sang softly as she came up to him. Then, before she could ask him what he meant, he said, "Looks like you gave him something to think about."

She glanced back at Rab; he was still standing there, looking as if he didn't believe what he'd just heard.

"Rab isn't used to being stood up to," Jon said with relish. "Oh, my, it's going to be an interesting year. But you be careful, Katy, okay?" he said more seriously. "Once a bully . . ."

"I'll be careful."

They both ordered hot fudge sundaes—Kate had forgotten how enormous the Ice Cream Shack's sundaes were—and then, when Charlie Moss came up and suggested it, they went across the road to the skating pond. "I think you'll find a better class of people away from them," Charlie said, indicating Rab and his circle as they passed.

It was a quiet group by the pond: Kate's old seatmate, Marcia Brooks, and her friend Carol, plus Ricky Jarvis and a number of people from the band and the theater group, with a few from a computer club called "The Basic Bytes" thrown in. "Welcome," said Ricky, who was one of the Basic Bytes, holding out a joint in his plump hand.

Kate shook her head and without comment Ricky handed the joint to Jon, who drew on it deeply and passed it along. "So," said Ricky, "what do you think now that you've seen more of us?"

Kate laughed. "If one more person asks me that," she said, for many had in the few days she'd been at school, "I think I'll probably scream." She scraped the last of her hot fudge out of the bottom of her plastic cup. "Or bash someone's head in."

"Wow," said Marcia. "Is this the kid who walked away peacefully when someone in this very group pulled her hair?"

"Did I?" asked Kate.

"You sure did," Ricky told her, laughing. "I was so mad you didn't react I almost cried."

"You did cry," said Charlie, pointing at Ricky. "I saw you—and gloated, little creep that I was."

"Gee, Ricky," Kate said, fluttering her eyelids in a passable imitation of a twenties flapper she'd seen in a movie with Chelsea back in Providence, "I didn't know you cared."

"Oh, I did, I did," Ricky said. "With—what was it? Fourth-grade passion." Everyone laughed and Ricky reached out and touched Kate's shoulder. "Hey, it's good to have you back. Makes our old class complete again. Rounds it out nicely."

"Sure does," said Charlie, sculpting a buxom female figure in the air with his hands, and everyone laughed again, a little embarrassed this time, though. Jon glanced at Kate, but she joined in the laughter, not minding. Charlie had always been able to get away with personal jokes that would hurt coming from anyone else; it would be impossible to interpret his gesture as anything but friendly and flattering. If it had been Rab, now . . .

But Rab was nowhere in sight, and Kate settled back near Jon, leaning against him and enjoying the feeling of being part of her old class again.

· · ·

Later, Jon walked Kate home, both of them alternately singing and joking, playing Miss Kettle and Mr. Pot.

"We ought to be quiet," Kate said in an exaggerated whisper as they crossed the common.

"It's only ten-thirty," said Jon in a normal voice.

"Yeah, but look." Kate pointed to the silent houses. "No lights." She pointed down, widening her eyes in mock surprise. "No sidewalks either. I guess they still roll them up at ten o'clock."

"Oh, they do, they do," Jon answered, straight-faced. "Keeps 'em cleaner, don'cha know?" They crossed the street; when they reached the curb they both pretended to step over a rolled-up section of sidewalk and then to walk on rough ground, elaborately stumbling over imaginary rocks and falling against each other till they reached the Kincaids' front gate.

"What's that?" Jon asked as they opened the gate.

"What?"

He pointed to a shape by the driveway. "That."

Kate's heart nearly stopped. "It looks like someone lying down," she said. "Like a drunk or something."

Jon had already gone to the dark figure and was kneeling beside it. "Kate," he called urgently, "get your folks, it's Dan."

"Oh, my God," Kate said, not trying to be quiet any longer. She ran up the steps and pounded on the door, then fumbled for her key. The house was empty. "They must still be at the meeting," she said, coming out again and going to the garage. "Yes. Dad's car's gone."

"Is your mother's car there?" asked Jon, wiping blood off Dan's head with the napkin from his sundae.

"No," said Kate; she knew Dan had taken it earlier.

She kneeled by his side, next to Jon. "Dan?" she asked tentatively, touching his cheek. "Dan?"

Dan's eyelids fluttered. "Katy," he said. "Thank God." Then he groaned.

"Easy, man," said Jon. "Don't try to move just yet. Where do you hurt?"

"Oh, God, all over," said Dan, struggling to sit up. "No—no," he said as Jon tried to make him lie back, but he leaned against Jon anyway. "It's okay. Just a little —dizzy."

"What happened?" asked Kate.

Dan shook his head, then grabbed it with both hands and held it, groaning again. "I was coming home from Cambridge. Mom's car—oh, lord, the car . . ." He sat up sharply, and tried to stand.

"Never mind the car," said Jon, forcing him back and keeping one arm around his shoulders. "It's you we're worried about. We've got to get you some help. Katy . . ."

"Hospital," said Kate, snapping to her senses. "I'll call an ambulance—or—or—who does one call, Jon?"

"Fire department or cops," said Jon.

Dan held up his hand. "Don't need an ambulance. Costs too much. Let's just drive there."

"There's no car," said Jon. "Your dad's car isn't here."

"Mom's is somewhere by the bridge," Dan said thickly. "Let's go get it." Again he tried to stand.

"Look, Dan," said Jon, gently pulling him back. "You shouldn't go anywhere except the hospital. I could get the car, but it would probably take longer than for an ambulance to get here."

" 'S okay," Dan said fuzzily.

"No," Kate heard herself tell him firmly. "Jon's right. It'll be faster to call for help. You said yourself you're dizzy. Shut up," she ordered as he started to object again, and she ran into the dark house and fumbled for the police number. "This is Kate Kincaid," she said into the phone, trying to sound calm. "Forty-seven Main Street. My brother's been hurt. My parents are out and there's no car here. Can someone help us get an ambulance?"

"Be right over," said a kind voice. "Sit tight, Kate, okay? Is he conscious?"

"Yes, sort of."

"Broken bones, blood?"

"I—I don't know about the bones. There's some blood on his head."

"Well, you just keep him still till we get there. Won't be but a minute. Someone's already on the way."

As she hung up, Kate realized she was trembling —or shivering; she felt cold. Then she remembered that people in shock feel cold, too, so she ran upstairs, grabbed a blanket from her bed, and brought it down, tucking it carefully around her brother, who she was glad to see was at least sitting quietly now, supported by Jon. Dan's eyes were closed and he looked as if he was trying very hard not to cry. She took his hand and held it as tightly as she could.

"It's okay, Katy," he said weakly, sounding very far away. "I'm okay. It's just this lousy—headache. And . . ."

"And?" prompted Jon, shifting slightly, but still bracing him.

"Hurts to talk," said Dan. "And breathe." He passed his hand over his chest.

"Ribs," said Jon softly. "I bet. Stay still."

Then there was a siren and flashing lights, and a police cruiser followed by an ambulance pulled into the driveway. Two emergency medical technicians jumped out of the ambulance and loaded Dan onto a stretcher, moving him swiftly and deftly, but not so smoothly that he didn't groan again, especially when they straightened him out so that he was lying flat. "Sorry, son," said one of the EMTs.

"You his sister?" asked the other. "You Kate?"

Kate nodded.

"Better come along with us," said the EMT. "He'll feel better if there's someone with him he knows."

Both Kate and Jon rode in the ambulance, and two police officers followed in the cruiser to make out a report as soon as Dan was able to talk to them.

But by the time they all got to the hospital, which was on the border of Hastings Bay and the next town, Warton, Dan had passed out again.

9

IT WASN'T UNTIL the next morning that Kate finally heard the whole story. By that time she and her parents had been at the hospital for hours—the police had gotten her parents out of the meeting—and the doctors had X-rayed and examined Dan and said that he had a mild-to-moderate concussion, a cut and bruised head but no skull fracture, and three broken ribs. They'd given him a shot to forestall infection and put him to bed, saying the other Kincaids could stay till he came to.

It was about 6 A.M. when a nurse appeared in the waiting room where Kate and her mother were dozing; her father was with Dan. "Your son's awake now, Mrs. Kincaid," said the nurse, shaking Mom gently. "He'd like to see you."

Kate and her mother scrambled to their feet and hurried through the dimly lit corridors to Dan's room.

He looked pale, but a lot better, propped up a bit on his pillows, tape around his chest and reddish-brown antiseptic on his forehead where one of his many bruises wore an ugly ragged scrape.

"Hi," said Mom, instantly cheerful, bending over to kiss him.

Kate tried to match her mother's cheerfulness, but it was hard being back in a hospital room again after all those anxious weeks when Dad had been in intensive care and then in the cardiac unit; it was as if she'd never left.

"Hi," said Dan. "Hey, I'm sorry, everyone."

"He's done nothing but apologize since he woke up," said Dad, who was holding Dan's hand. "I try to tell him he's a darn fool, but he won't listen."

"Well," said Mom, winking at Dad and Kate, "you know what the doctor said about concussions. The patient may behave erratically for the first forty-eight hours. May be unreasonable, highly emotional, all that."

"Oh, don't make me laugh, Mama," said Dan. "My ribs hurt."

"How's your head?" asked Kate.

"Looks as thick as ever," said Dad affectionately. "Sore, too, I bet—sorehead."

Dan smiled. "Mom, the car," he said. "I think it's okay. It's on the Hastings Bay side of the bridge, sort of by the woods there. There's a dirt road down to the river; I'd pulled into that . . ."

"The car's fine," said Dad. "The police took it back to the house last night. Not a scratch on it, they told me. Which rules out a car accident," he said, looking narrowly at Dan. "Right?"

"Right," said Dan. He took a deep breath, then let it out, wincing again. "It's a weird story," he said. "I still don't quite get it."

Something in his voice made Kate's stomach turn leaden.

"I was driving home," he said, "about dusk, at least it was still a little light. You're going to think I'm crazy, but I heard this cat sound or something in the woods. I thought maybe there was some animal hurt, you know, had gotten hit by a car and had crawled into the woods? Then I thought, babies sound like cats sometimes and it might even be a baby, abandoned or something. So I drove a bit onto the dirt road and then went into the woods on foot, calling"—he cleared his throat self-consciously—"'Kitty, kitty, kitty,' I'm afraid, because it seemed more likely for it to be a cat."

Kate suppressed a smile; it was just like Dan to go after a hurt animal, but it was hard not to be amused at the picture of all six foot one of him going through the woods calling "Kitty, kitty, kitty."

"So I got to where I couldn't see the road anymore —I think I was near the riverbank, because it was kind of open, or beginning to be—and—and these four guys, maybe my age, maybe a little younger, suddenly were right there in front of me."

Dan rubbed his hand over his head. Their father, Kate could see, was leaning forward and Mom was watching him—Dad—nervously.

"Then they started saying things, taunting, sort of, about my calling 'Kitty, kitty.' I can't blame them; it was pretty silly. I tried to laugh it off. Then one of them said, 'Look, who are you? This here's private property.' I remember that; he said 'this here's.' I'm pretty sure it's not private property, but I didn't think the guy who spoke would take well to contradicting, so I told him my name. And then one of the others said, 'River View, huh?' and the first one said"—here Dan glanced at Kate—"'You got a sister named Kate?—a meddling sister,' I think he said, or something like that, anyway."

Out of the corner of her eye, Kate saw her mother look at her questioningly; Kate turned away.

"I said I did have a sister Kate, and then they all started talking at once. The gist of what they said was that it was time we both learned not to mess around with Hastings Bay people—and then they jumped me. With four of them," he said apologetically, "there wasn't a whole lot I could do."

"Of course not," said Dad. "Of course not." He patted Dan's shoulder. "Did you recognize any of them, son? Hear any names, anything like that?"

"No," said Dan. "Sorry. Nothing."

"And they just left you?" said Mom, her face still showing the horror that had grown in it as Dan had told his story. "Hurt you and left you there?"

Dan shifted position, then winced once more and leaned back against the pillows. "I guess they just left me there," he said. "I remember falling but I must've hit my head on a rock or something because I don't remember anything after that till it was dark and I was alone and the stars were out. I couldn't find the car—I don't think I could've driven it anyway—but I did finally find Route 40 and crawled home. And then I guess I passed out again in the driveway."

"Do you mean to say," said Dad, "that you crawled all that way and not a single car saw you and stopped to help? Good lord, son, it's . . ."

"Not too many cars went by," said Dan, reaching for the water glass beside his bed. Kate handed it to him; he took it gratefully and drank. "And," he went on, handing the glass back to her, "when cars did go by, I lay flat so they wouldn't see me. I didn't know but what those guys would come looking for me if they went back and saw I'd left."

"Oh, you probably scared them off for good by passing out," said Dad. "I don't suppose you remember anything about what they looked like or what they were wearing?"

"It was almost dark," said Dan, "as I said." He turned to Kate. "What did they mean about you?" he asked.

"Yes, Kate," said Mom, "what did they mean? Do you have any idea who they might have been?"

"I'm not sure who they were," said Kate reluctantly, "but I guess what they meant, you know, about meddling, was—I guess they don't think I should be friends with Pippa."

"Since when," said Dad, "is being friends with someone a crime?"

"Since—I don't really know," said Kate, and she explained the feud as best she could.

"I remember," Dan said, in the shocked silence that followed, "back when I was in junior high, whenever there was trouble people would say, 'Oh, must be Hastings Bay kids.' It seemed funny at the time, sort of. I mean, it was obvious it couldn't always be them."

Mom cleared her throat, as if it was hard for her to speak. "Of course not," she said.

"That kind of rivalry exists in lots of towns," said Dad. "Factions resenting each other, blaming each other. But something like this . . ." He got up. "It's time I called the police," he said. "They've been waiting to hear what happened anyway."

And he stalked furiously out of Dan's room.

. . .

Kate felt conspicuous walking into school later that day—suspicious, too, for she was certain the boys who had beaten Dan up went to the high school and were from Hastings Bay. And that means, she thought, that I'm being forced to become part of the feud myself; at least I bet that's what they want.

She made a special effort to seem friendly to everyone, most of all to Pippa, who seemed awkward and restrained when she said how sorry she was about Dan. That made Kate wonder more than she already had if Pippa's brother Nick had had anything to do with it.

By lunchtime she was obsessed with the idea of talking to him. Even if he hadn't taken part in the beating, she reasoned, if he really is some kind of leader, he must know about it.

In the cafeteria, Kate avoided her own friends and went over to the table where the toughest Hastings Bay students usually sat—mostly seniors but a few juniors, Skid Johnson among them.

"Hi," she said, trying to ignore the hostility in the six pairs of eyes that surveyed her. "Is one of you Nick Brown?"

Skid leaned over and whispered something to the boy next to him.

"Maybe," said the boy Skid had spoken to. "Is one of you Kate Kincaid?"

"All of us," said Kate promptly. At least they snickered.

"My sister's right," said a squarely built, self-assured-looking boy on the other side of the table. He tipped back his chair, giving Kate the impression of coiled muscles, ready to spring. He had Pippa's curly hair—darker and shorter, but just as unruly—and the look in his eyes was noncommittal, cautious, certainly not offering the instant friendship Pippa's had. "You've got guts," he said, "and"—he smiled, not unpleasantly—"you've got class."

"Thank you," Kate said brightly, wanting to disappear. "Um—I'd like to talk to you? Privately, for a minute."

"Whoooo-*eeee!*" shouted Skid, slapping the table. "Man, I dunno about these River View women! Just come right out and say it, don't they? *River View woman.*" He sang the line as if it were "St. Louis woman."

"I said talk," said Kate sharply, cutting him off. "And that's what I meant—talk."

"Baby," said Skid, with an air of assumed sympathy, "any woman who goes around with a wimp like Jon Westgate must want a little more than talk."

Kate gritted her teeth. "Any woman who goes around with an animal like some of the ones at this table," she said brashly, "must have forgotten *how* to talk. Baby." So far, so good, Katy, she told herself as Nick silenced Skid and stood up, putting a casual hand in the small of her back. "Let's go," he said. "Animals is right," he called over his shoulder at his friends, who whistled as he guided Kate out of the cafeteria and into the hall.

There he blocked her way by putting one hand on the wall beside her and leaning on it. "What is it you want to talk about? Aren't you coming to my house for dinner this week anyway?"

"Yes," said Kate carefully, "but my brother was beaten up last night in Hastings Bay, right by the bridge. That doesn't seem much like dinner conversation. Besides, Thursday's a long time to wait to find out if you know anything about it. Do you?"

Nick's eyes narrowed. "Maybe I do," he said. "And maybe I don't. Just what was your brother doing walking around our woods?"

"Oh," said Kate quickly. "So you do know."

"I said maybe," Nick answered, unperturbed. "Just what was he doing?"

"I don't see that it's any of your business," said Kate, bristling in spite of trying not to. "As far as I know, the woods by each side of the river belong to the town or the state, certainly not to any kid in either town."

"Kids," said Nick, "have parents, and parents own land. At least the kids in Hastings Bay have parents. I don't know about the ones in River View. Maybe you people make babies in bottles."

Kate fought the urge to walk away. "My brother thought he heard a cat or a child crying. So he did what any decent human being would do. He got out of his car to look, in case something or someone was hurt. But he was jumped on and beaten up. I call that pretty rotten."

Nick's mouth tightened. "I call it pretty rotten, too," he said, "if it's true. The way I heard it, your brother was crashing around trying to find the boat launch. The boat launch is private."

"The boat launch," said Kate, "is not private. I do know that much. It belongs to the town, just like the one in River View does."

"Yeah, so the one on our side belongs to the town of Hastings Bay, for the use of Hastings Bay residents. As you said, you've got your own boat launch on your own side."

"We don't beat people up who walk on our side," said Kate, now letting her anger show.

"Oh, no?" said Nick, also angrily. "Well, maybe you're just still too new here to know about that. Listen, the other night one of our men had a certain need when he was on the View side of the river. Now this man had had a few beers and he'd been driving a long way, and he realized he wasn't going to make it home. So he stopped and went into the woods to—ah—relieve himself. And he ended up in the hospital, too. Only he didn't have to stay there so he went back to River View the next night to make it clear he knew that his rights, shall we say, had been violated. But that time he met up with some River View cops who had their own ideas about his rights—like he didn't have any, to them. An eye for an eye, baby. It's the only way to survive. See you Thursday." With that, Nick strode back into the cafeteria.

"So it is true," Kate said to Jon later, "that a Hastings Bay kid got beaten up by View kids just recently?"

They were on the View side of the river, at their old frogging place.

"Skid," said Jon. "By Rab and his pals. And what I heard today was that the next night when he went back looking for Rab the River View cops stopped him for loitering or something and told him not to come back."

"Damn," said Kate angrily, realizing that Skid's account of the same incident must have been what she'd overheard at the bonfire. "How can the cops do that?"

"When it comes to kids," Jon said, "the cops on both sides are often a little hasty. Both sides appointed youth officers after the accident with Gilda. They're supposed to know how to deal with kids, but they haven't done much yet. And I guess it wasn't our youth officer who ran into Skid when he came back here. Even if the youth officers haven't done much, they're not dumb."

"It's not fair to say that someone can't even drive through town," Kate said. "Or stop in town. It sounds to me as if the cops are part of the problem."

"Some cops," said Jon. "And some kids. Not all of either. Circles," he said softly. "It goes in never-ending circles, drawing tighter and tighter."

"Then someone's got to loosen the string," said Kate, more determined than ever.

"As nearly as I can figure out, it's getting worse," Kate said to Dan the next day in the hospital sun room after she'd given him a batch of crossword puzzles and told him about Skid's being beaten up in River View. "And I want to stop it, Dan. It's got to end before more people like you get hurt."

"Listen to you," Dan said mildly. "It's like when you were little and you first heard about some dictator or other and wanted to go bump him off all by yourself."

"It was Hitler," said Kate, remembering right away. "And it wasn't that I wanted to bump him off; I knew he was dead. But I didn't understand why no one else had done it, since everyone said he was bad. That's before I became a pacifist like Mom," she added.

"Everyone *you* knew thought he was bad," said Dan. "But not everyone. Things aren't as simple as you make them, Katy."

She hesitated. "I know. But—but I also don't know.

When something's right, doesn't one have to act on it? You always have. Like the draft, about signing up."

"That's different," said Dan. "And it's a bad example. You think one thing about that; I think another—so who's right? Besides, that's just a one-person thing, the draft, at least in that what I do or don't do just has to do with me. But your thing isn't; it's a lot of people."

Kate got up and looked out the window. A woman with a baby in her arms was being helped out of a wheelchair and into a car. "I still keep thinking," she said as the car drove off, "that if everyone got to know each other more, if there were more things for kids to do together . . . Dan, there's not even a movie theater till you get all the way to Warton."

Dan laboriously got up and joined her at the window, leaning against its frame as if he were dizzy, facing her. "Noble aim," he said. "But the thing is that the stuff you'll think of to do probably won't be the stuff the kids who are making trouble will be interested in."

"How about—I don't know. Macho things. Motorcycle races, things like that?"

"Here?" said Dan incredulously, going back to his chair. "Where here? On the roads? Oh, the cops'll love that! Not to mention the good citizens of River View."

"Bike races, then."

"Katy, Katy, any creep like Rab who wants to show off on a motorcycle isn't going to want to race a regular bike. Bikes are for little kids, or wimps, to him."

Kate sighed and sat down next to him. "I guess you're right. Something else, then."

"*What* else?" he said. "Jeez, look at who you're dealing with! Does Rab strike you as a reasonable person? Or that guy Skid? They're way past paying attention to anyone who doesn't agree with them, Katy, especially —forgive me—especially if that person's a girl."

"Oh, come on."

"I'm serious." He rubbed his forehead. "Learn how to fight, at least," he said abruptly. "If you're going to try to reason with those creeps. I mean fistfight kind of fighting."

She stared at him.

"Karate," he said insistently. "Something like that. One of those self-defense courses for women. Maybe you and Pippa could both take one. After all, she'll be just about as vulnerable as you if you try to interfere. Maybe even more."

🞋 10

WEDNESDAY Dan got out of the hospital, and Thursday, after his first classes at Harvard, he insisted on driving Kate to Pippa's for dinner, despite their mother's objections. "I feel fine, Mom," he said. But Kate knew his health wasn't the only thing worrying Mom, and it wasn't the only thing worrying her either, she realized, annoyed at her own uneasiness as they crossed the bridge and drove along Route 40 on the Hastings Bay side.

"Enemy territory," quipped Dan. "But I thought that this morning, too, and coming home, and it was okay."

Kate knew he was trying to reassure her, but Nick's ominous "See you Thursday" was still very much in her mind, and she was close to wishing she'd made up some excuse and stayed home. But how could she even begin to accomplish anything without at least trying to include Nick?

The Browns' house was about two miles from the bridge, but still on the flood plain, for the river curved in around Hastings after passing the regional school. Though the house looked freshly painted, Kate was sure its yard and cellar were wet in the spring; the faint dark line a foot or so up on its foundation looked like a water stain so permanent no paint could quite cover it.

"Well," said Kate nervously as Dan stopped, "thanks for the ride."

"Glad to do it. Have a good time."

"You be careful," she said, opening the door. "No getting out of the car on the way back."

"More to the point," he said, "you call if you need a ride home. I'll be in all night." He patted the pile of newly purchased books that lay on the seat between them. "And every night for the next four years, looks like," he added. "Get, now. Someone's looking out at you."

As Kate turned after waving Dan off, she could see thin white curtains pulled slightly apart at a window to the left of the door, and a shadowy face, low down, as if it were a child's. She went up the neat flagstone walk, bordered with fading red flowers, and rang the bell.

Pippa came to the door, a little pale girl in pigtails half hidden behind her.

"Hi, Katy," she said, easy and cheerful; Kate began to relax. Even if Nick was the point of this dinner, Pippa was going to be there, too, after all.

"This is Cassie," Pippa said, pushing the child, who must have been around four, forward. "Say hello, Cas. This is my friend Kate."

Kate knelt, smiling. "Hi, Cassie," she said. "How are you?"

"My kitty had kitties," Cassie said proudly, removing her thumb from her mouth just long enough to get the words out. "Want to see?"

Pippa laughed. "She must like you," she said. "Those kittens are mighty special."

"I'd love to see them," said Kate, getting up and taking

the hand Cassie held out to her. "I love kitties," she said, as Cassie, Pippa following, led her down a darkish hall to the right of a staircase. "I had a kitty myself once but she got run over."

Cassie turned huge dark eyes up to Kate and said, "You could have one of mine, then, 'kay, Pippy? When they get bigger, 'kay?"

"We'll have to ask Mommy," said Pippa. "And Kate will have to ask her mother. They just moved here, Cassie; maybe they're too busy."

"For a *kitty?*" Cassie asked scornfully, leading Kate into the kitchen and opening what appeared to be the cellar door.

As she turned, Kate could see steam rising from an old gas stove and a woman, scarf around her head and apron around her waist, standing at it, stirring. "Shouldn't we . . . ?" she said to Pippa.

"Right," Pippa answered. "Mom," she said, "here's Kate. Cassie wants to show her the kittens."

"That Cassie," the woman said fondly, wiping her hands on her apron and turning with tired eyes to Kate. "She thinks everyone loves cats as much as she. How do you do, Kate? I'm so glad you could come. The men'll be here in a few minutes—Nick and his father are down at the station, still." She gave a worried glance at the clock on the flowered wall. "I told them six-thirty sharp."

"They'll be here, Mom," soothed Pippa, and Kate got the impression that one of Pippa's main jobs was to keep her mother calm. "And if they're late—well, Kate won't mind, will you, Kate?"

"No, of course not," said Kate, shaking Mrs. Brown's outstretched hand; it was small and a little rough, but

100

with beautifully kept, rounded nails. "Hello, Mrs. Brown. Thank you for inviting me."

"I hope spaghetti's okay," Mrs. Brown said. "And a green salad."

"My mother makes the best salads in the world," Pippa said. "I could almost live on them. Unfortunately, I don't."

"Spaghetti's wonderful," said Kate. "One of my favorites. And we don't have it all that much anymore; my dad has to watch his weight."

"They have this new spaghetti," said Mrs. Brown eagerly. "Low carbohydrate, all protein. Maybe he could have that. Of course, the sauce . . ."

"Mommy," said Cassie impatiently, tugging at Kate's hand. "She wants to see the kitties."

"Go, angel, go," said Mrs. Brown, running her hand swiftly over the child's hair. "I'll call you as soon as Nick and Daddy come, yes, Pippa?"

"Fine, Mom." Pippa opened a door at the far end of the kitchen, switched on a light, and stepped back for Cassie, who led Kate down steep stairs into a cellar that, although visibly dry, smelled strongly of mildew. Kate noticed a dehumidifier in the center of the floor.

Next to the oil burner there was a cardboard box, one end cut away, and there on an old blanket in a nest of shredded newspaper lay a beautiful calico cat, nursing eight tiny balls of multicolored fuzz. "Oh!" Kate exclaimed involuntarily, and dropped to her knees.

"They're having their supper," Cassie said gravely, "so you can't pick them up. But you could pat them —careful." Cassie demonstrated, reaching out a forefinger and gently stroking the rounded hump that seemed to be the largest kitten.

Kate did the same.

"They're only two weeks old," said Pippa, kneeling beside Kate, "so they don't really have personalities yet. But they're all strong and healthy, aren't they, Cassie, so we won't have any trouble giving them away."

"But we're keeping one," said Cassie firmly.

"Yes, we are, sweetheart."

"And I get to pick."

"That's right. The one you like best." Pippa had her arm around Cassie now. "Which do you think?"

Cassie put her head on one side, a miniature version of Pippa's similar gesture. "The black one, *may*be," she said. "But maybe the spotty one." She looked up at Kate. "You won't want those ones, will you?" she asked anxiously.

"Oh, no," said Kate quickly, "I won't. I won't decide till you've picked anyway, okay?"

" 'Kay," said Cassie, looking relieved.

"Girls!" came Mrs. Brown's voice down the stairs. "Supper's ready."

They went back up, and Kate, as Pippa pointed out the downstairs bathroom, got a glimpse of Nick standing awkwardly in the hall with a taller but equally stocky dark man—Mr. Brown, she realized. He looked very much like Nick except his face and body were more settled.

"It's okay, Pip," Kate said, refusing the bathroom. "Thanks." She went into the hall and tried hard to smile in a friendly way at Nick; he nodded curtly. "Hi, Nick," she said, ignoring that, then turned to the man beside him. "You must be Mr. Brown."

"Manners, Pippa," scolded Mrs. Brown, crossing the hall with a gravy boat brimming with tomato sauce.

"Dad, this is Kate Kincaid," said Pippa hastily, and then, as they all followed Mrs. Brown into the dining room, she whispered, "There'll be grace. I don't know if you say it at your house."

"No," Kate whispered back. "But I like it."

They sat around the table, Cassie on a pile of phone books next to Kate, with Nick—was he purposely avoiding her eyes?—and Pippa opposite her. Nick and his father looked ruddy, as if they'd just scrubbed their faces and hands at considerable risk to their skin—which I suppose they did, Kate thought as they all bowed their heads, since they were working at the gas station.

"Cassie," said Mrs. Brown softly.

"Bless this food," piped Cassie, crossing herself a little unsurely, "that we are—um—to eat and thank you for —it and for our kitties and for our new friend, Kate. In the name of the-father-the-son-and-the-holy-spi-rit," she finished quickly, rolling most of the words into one, while crossing herself again, as did the others. Then she opened her eyes and looked anxiously at her mother. " 'Kay?' she asked in a loud whisper.

"Perfect," said Mrs. Brown, dishing out spaghetti, handing a full plate to her husband via Nick, who'd applauded; Cassie beamed at him.

Mr. Brown reached for the sauce and said, "We hear lots about you these days, Kate. Sauce?"

Kate said, "Yes, please," and watched him carefully

ladle sauce over the heaping plate of spaghetti that she now realized was intended for her.

"Plenty of sauce," he said, handing her the plate, "to keep the spaghetti hot and slide it down nice and easy." He drew out the words "plenty" and "slide," and Pippa and Nick chuckled as if at a longstanding family joke; Cassie went into gales of laughter.

"Thank you," said Kate. "It looks wonderful."

"My wife's family," said Mr. Brown, "is Italian, and she's just about converted me. Except for roast beef and Yorkshire pudding. That's one English taste I'll never lose."

The spaghetti was indeed delicious, the salad even more so, and Kate found herself eating with a gusto she never thought she'd show outside her own family. For a while, conversation was limited to school, the weather, and Cassie's kittens; everyone seemed too concentrated on the food to be able to handle anything more complicated.

"So," said Mr. Brown, looking Kate's way when they had finished and Pippa and Cassie were clearing the table; Mrs. Brown said she wouldn't hear of Kate's helping "this first time," which made Kate feel even more welcome than she already did. "So," said Mr. Brown again, "how do your folks find River View after four years away?"

"Oh, they're very happy to be back," Kate answered, explaining about her father's heart attack and ending by saying, "They both love gardening, and you can't do much of that in the city. At least not on the scale they like to do it."

"Too bad it's so late in the year, then," said Mr.

Brown, "but if your dad's like me, he gardens all year round in his mind anyway." He cleared his throat. "What does he think of this waste-disposal thing?" he asked after a glance at his wife. "I understand they had a meeting about it the other night over in River View. We don't have ours till next week."

"Oh?" said Kate, surprised. "Are you meeting about it, too? That's—that's very nice of you," she added lamely.

"Nice!" exploded Nick, who had spoken less than anyone since the beginning of the meal but who had put away two and a half plates of spaghetti. "Since it'll probably end up over here, there's nothing much nice about it."

"Nick!" admonished Mrs. Brown. "What a thing to say!"

"Well, it's true," said Nick.

"Why would it end up here?" asked Kate, bewildered, looking from Nick to his father. "I thought it was supposed to be on our side . . ." She stopped, cringing, hearing herself say "our side," and then for a moment blamed Nick for forcing her into it.

But he didn't, she told herself; you said it yourself, as if it were perfectly natural.

"Might be on your side," said Mr. Brown, pushing his chair back from the table and folding his napkin, "might not be. But I'll have to agree with Nick that with the two sites picked out, chances are it'll end up here. No offense, but Hastings Bay doesn't have the resources to fight that kind of thing that you—that River View has."

I'm not the only one being careful, thought Kate; then Nick said bluntly, "Money is what Dad means by resources."

For the second time Kate was angry at Nick, but aloud she said, "I didn't even know there were two sites."

Mr. Brown looked startled. "Your folks didn't say?"

"They didn't say much about the meeting," Kate said apologetically. "I haven't talked to them much—really any—about it. You see, my brother's been in the hospital, and . . ."

"Oh, dear," said Mrs. Brown. "I'm sorry to hear that. Nothing serious, I hope?"

"He was be—" Pippa began.

"No, nothing serious," Kate interrupted, drowning her out. "And he's okay now."

"Well, that must be a relief to your parents. It's hard having a child in the hospital." She reached over and tugged one of Cassie's pigtails. "Run up, now, honey, and I'll come in a minute and tuck you in."

"I want her to tuck me in," Cassie said, pointing to Kate.

"No, dear, I'm sure Kate wants to talk to Pippa. She's Pippa's friend, after all."

Cassie's face crumpled and Kate quickly said, "It's okay, Mrs. Brown, I'd love to." She turned to Cassie. "I don't have a little sister, so you'll have to show me how to do it right."

" 'Kay," Cassie said, climbing down off her chair. "First you stay here till I call you. *Then* you come up."

"Okay." Kate watched her go. "She's so cute," she said to Mrs. Brown when Cassie was out of the room.

"Yes, she's a great joy to us," said Mrs. Brown, standing, picking up the coffeepot. But something in her voice made Kate think just the opposite was true, or was also true.

Later, Kate asked Pippa about it, when she joined her in her room after reading Cassie a story and giving goodnight kisses to her and the two dolls and one stuffed cat who slept with her. Pippa said, so matter-of-factly Kate knew it was anything but, "Cassie's got leukemia. I know she seems okay but that's because she's in remission."

"Oh, Pippa," Kate said, stunned, reaching out to her. "How awful for you! For all of you—for Cassie . . ."

Pippa smiled wanly. "It's okay a lot of the time," she said. "We're sort of used to it, I guess. It's just when she's *not* in remission . . . Come on, let's find Nick." She smiled, more broadly now. "After all, he's why you came, right?"

"Right," said Kate with forced brightness, trying to hide the nervousness that instantly possessed her. "At least part of why." She touched Pippa's hand. "It was good meeting your folks, and Cassie, and seeing where you live."

Pippa pressed Kate's hand briefly, and led her downstairs.

They found Nick on the porch, and Pippa, after rather awkwardly offering to get some lemonade, left them.

"So," said Nick from where he sat on the porch railing in the semidarkness, "you're Jon Westgate's girl, I hear?"

Kate gave a startled laugh and said, "Everyone sure seems to want to think so."

"You mean you're not?"

"I mean," said Kate, "that Jon and I have known each other since we were six, and are very close."

"Ummm," said Nick. "So you might be more brother and sister than boyfriend-girlfriend, but you're not sure. That what you mean?"

"I guess. Look, that's not what I came here to . . ."

"Yeah," said Nick. "I know." He reached into his pocket—Kate again thought of muscles ready to spring —and pulled out a pack of cigarettes, shaking it sharply until a few popped up; he offered her the pack.

She shook her head.

Nick pulled a cigarette out with his lips, replaced the pack, and silently lit up, holding the match facing his palm as he struck it, so that his hand cupped the flame when it blazed. What theatrical props, Kate thought, mildly annoyed. But she knew she liked watching him move, all the same.

"You came here tonight," Nick said, throwing his head back to inhale, "waving a truce flag, like what's between Hastings and River View's a kids' game of cops and robbers, like it's fun. Right?"

"I came here," Kate said carefully, "first of all because I'm Pippa's friend. And I also came here because she thought I might be able to talk to you. That is, I . . ."

"So," interrupted Nick, "so talk." He put his hands on either side of his head, pushing his ears forward. "I've got big ears. Talk, Peacemaker."

Kate drew a deep breath, thinking wryly that at least that was a better nickname than her old one. "It's just that the whole thing seems—childish," she said, then hoped he wouldn't find the word insulting. She went on quickly, to cover. "And dangerous, too. I've been trying to find out how it started, but it seems to me that no one remembers, and if that's true, how it started can't matter anymore. Now it's just people hating each other on principle, only I guess for the last few years it's gotten a lot worse." She took another deep breath. "Branding people, for instance."

"So that's it."

"No," said Kate. "No, it isn't. It could be if I let it, but it isn't. And that was—that was between View and View anyway, even if it did have to do with being friends with someone from Hastings. No, it's the way one thing keeps leading to another, to a worse thing. Gilda," she said tentatively, trying to see his reaction—but it had grown too dark. "I know about that. And I know it wasn't your fault."

Nick's cigarette glowed brighter, but he said nothing.

"But," Kate went on, "with things the way they are, I guess most View kids blame you for it. Especially Rab, since he went out with her." Kate paused; still no reaction. "After Gilda I guess there were lots of small things, and now there's—Skid, wasn't it?—getting beaten up, and then my brother. The thing is, what's going to happen next? And if it goes on and on, what's going to happen in the end?"

He was silent for such a long time, his cigarette glowing and fading as he puffed on it, that Kate was afraid he wasn't going to say anything. But then he stubbed the cigarette out on the porch railing and said, astonishing her, "What's going to happen in the end is out of our hands. Out of mine, out of yours. And it's a heck of a lot worse than anything we could do to each other. So, Peacemaker," he said, walking over to her and looking down, "you're too late. What happens next doesn't matter because the damn waste dump, one way or another, will probably finish us all off."

✣ II

AGAIN she couldn't sleep; her mind wouldn't let her rest. Finally, she got up and went to the small desk that stood by the window in her room, looking out at the September stars, trying to organize her thoughts and feelings into a poem.

But nothing emerged that was coherent enough to write down.

To her amazement, Nick had asked her to go out with him the next Saturday night, and to her equal amazement, she had accepted.

She still didn't know why; to find out more—his motives, maybe. Or because she liked him in spite of herself, was drawn to him. But it was in a way that disturbed her and made her mistrust herself—him, too—and made her feel disloyal, unloving, to Jon.

He *is* good-looking, she thought, going back to the bed and switching on her bedside light; there's no denying that.

"Dear Chelsea," she wrote in her mind, for want of anyone else to write to, "I have met a boy, a senior, who is a real macho-brute type, on the outside anyway, and who has asked me out, lord knows why, but who I don't think I like. He's the leader, in a way, of . . ."

But was he?

Did the kids in Hastings Bay who'd beaten Dan up even have a leader?

Well, she told herself again, turning off her light and getting back under the covers, maybe that *is* why I'm going out with him: to find that out.

By the time Saturday came she was so numb with thinking about her date and examining her feelings that she felt woozy. Jon had given her a strange look when she'd told him, but hadn't said anything; Pippa had patted her shoulder and said, "Have a good time, but keep an eye on him"; Marcia Brooks, somehow finding out about it, had said, "Good lord, be careful! Why not pick Rab if that's the type you want? At least Rab's from our side." Even so, she'd felt secret envy from some River View girls—silly, she'd thought, but she was also aware she enjoyed the feeling of status it gave her, and the feeling of adventure, of daring to trespass on forbidden territory.

"I am," she told herself aloud, surveying herself in the mirror as Nick's car drove up, "going to be whoever I want to be tonight. A *femme fatale*—Mata Hari—sophisticated—confident . . ."

But her mouth was dry as she went down the stairs and she found herself longing for Jon, or for Pippa to stand there on the sidelines and cheer her on. Judith, she thought, remembering the story of the Jewish widow who had offered herself to the enemy general Holofernes, in order to save her people; Judith going to the other side's leader.

Yes, but Judith killed Holofernes. And she was a *real* heroine.

Then she saw Nick below her in the hall, talking in a quite ordinary way to her parents, looking neat and —oh, lord, very handsome, very powerful—in a white polo shirt and newish jeans.

"Katy," he said, as she came the rest of the way down, "you look great."

She smiled self-consciously, glad that Pippa had suggested she wear a skirt; they were going, Nick had told her, to a party, at least for a while, at the house of a friend of his.

Nick held out his hands to her and then, with a quick goodbye to her parents, hurried her out the door and into the car; she just caught the edge of her father's frown as they left.

Of course Dad's nervous, she said to herself, as Nick shut the passenger door and went around to his side; it's my first real date.

So'm I, she thought, suppressing a desire to giggle; Mata Hari, indeed!

"So, Peacemaker," Nick said easily, as if he were used to nervous girls sitting next to him, "ready for a good time?"

Kate swallowed hard. "Sure."

"Me, too," he said, turning on the ignition. "Let's get this rig out of here so we can start." He swerved the car silently but too fast around the Common and sped out onto Route 40, crossing the bridge and then turning right. Abruptly he pulled into a side road and stopped in a place where there were no houses. "Hang on, Peacemaker," he said, getting out and going around behind the car. "Be right back."

Kate watched in the rearview mirror as he opened

the trunk and then closed it again. He got back into the car with two beers, and made great show of snapping the tops off. "Figured you could do with a little before we got to the party," he said, "seeing as how you don't know anyone there. Cheers." He tipped his beer up, chugalugging, then watched, clearly amused, while she took a slow swallow, stifled a burp, and swallowed again.

"Been drinking long?" he asked, chuckling, then shook his head. "Wrong," he said. "Wrong thing to say."

"No," said Kate, suddenly calm. "No, I haven't. But" —she forced a smile—"it's good. Thank you."

He looked at her, then shook his head once more. "You're welcome," he said, starting the car again. "You're very welcome. Nicholas," he said, pulling out onto the road—Hastings Bay's counterpart of River Road, running along the east bank—"you are out with a lady!"

She couldn't think of anything to say to that, and they drove in silence to the party, which was in a house roughly across the river from the high school, neat and well kept; unpretentious. The small rooms were crowded and hot, and there was more beer, plus several large jugs of wine and other things, too, Kate was sure, given the close, smoky atmosphere. There were too many people and too much noise for her to feel comfortable, though she played her part well, she thought, as she danced. She met several friends of Nick's who seemed open and warm—was that just because she was with him? Still, they didn't seem any more or less friendly than those of her River View classmates whom she didn't know well. Why, she wondered, dancing with a thin boy who reminded her a little of Jon, is it true that people are so much alike even when they think they're different?

Then Nick was beside her, cigarette dangling from his lips. He threw an arm across her shoulders, guiding her out of the room; he seemed quite a bit looser—drunker, she supposed—than before. "C'mon, sugar," he said, throwing his cigarette on the grass and crushing it under his foot. "We've put in our social call."

Outside in the car, fishing for his keys, he said, "See, Peacemaker? You've done your bit, now you can thank me."

"What do you mean?" Kate asked, suddenly cold, watching him trying to fit his key into the ignition.

"S'perfectly clear," he said, a little thickly, "isn't it? Why do you think I took you there? H'mm?"

"I—because a friend of yours was giving a party and you wanted to go to it."

"Wrong," he said. "So you could show the Hastings Bay kids that River View girls are okay. Just like you've been wanting to show them. And"—his eyes flashed triumphantly—"you did. You showed 'em. You danced fine and you drank fine and you talked fine. So step one's accomplished."

And then he was up against her on the car seat, putting his arms around her, groping for her lips with his.

Don't panic, she told herself; he's drunk and he did try to help; don't panic.

"Thank you," she said lightly, giving him a quick kiss and trying to push him away gently, annoyed that part of her was enjoying the contact with him even while she was resisting, and thinking with anger and disappointment that this certainly wasn't what she wanted her first kiss to be like.

"What's the matter?" he said. "Don't you like me?"

Oh, lord, she thought. "Of course I like you. But, Nick, you're—oh, damn, Nick, you're drunk," she said desperately, moving his hand away from the front of her blouse, hoping that wouldn't make him angry. "Come on, let's—let's get out and walk awhile. And maybe get you some coffee. Could we walk someplace? What's that place called? The Hut, isn't it?"

Nick fell back toward the driver's seat, laughing. "Walk to The Hut," he said. "Oh, God. Yeah, sure; sure, I guess we could walk to The Hut. Good idea. C'mon." He opened his door and got unsteadily out.

Relieved that he wasn't going to drive, she let him put his arm around her, mostly because she couldn't figure out how to avoid it—but it felt unthreatening, even pleasant. They walked along the river, back toward Route 40 and the bridge. He held her very close in the crook of his arm and she felt warmed by the sheer bulk of him, safe even though she sensed that she was the stronger, since he was drunk.

At the end of the road there was the bridge, and light from the bonfire dancing there.

"This way," he said, more soberly, leading her across the road. "Here's where the real people are. Let's see if you can show them, too."

"The Hut," said Kate. "After The Hut."

But now he wouldn't listen, and he propelled her roughly down the dirt road to the boat launch, reeling again. Is he really drunk, she wondered, or is he pretending?

The faces of his friends were distorted in the firelight, licked with tongues of light and shadow, reminding her of a painting she'd once seen of a witches' sabbat. But that's silly, she thought; there's no evil here, just kids, even if Skid is one of them—Skid and four or five other boys; two or three girls, too, sitting around the bonfire —sitting still, she realized, looking serious.

"Here," said Nick, pushing Kate forward, "here she is, the white dove of River View, the peacemaker. But looks like she's human, too." He held her tightly, one hand gripping each side of her waist. "She can dance and talk and drink and kiss; real flesh and blood—at least so far." He squeezed her, then slid his hands quickly down over her hips.

Suddenly she was terrified; she wanted to scream, to run, for he was handling her like merchandise and she saw that the eyes of some of the boys, Skid's especially, hardened. She glanced at the girls for help, but they looked away—or did she imagine it, there in the firelight? Oh, God, would they watch, would they even help, if . . .

But nothing happened, except that Nick glared at Skid when he came forward, and said "Bug off." Then with drunken dignity, Nick said, "Now, ladies and gentlemen, we are going to walk to The Hut because this lady has rightly pointed out to me that I am"—he burped —"a little under the weather."

"Table, you mean," Skid grumbled, slinking away, and there was laughter. One of the girls shot Kate what Kate took to be a sympathetic look and said softly, as if to reassure her, "It's not far."

"Thank you," Kate said gratefully, and then Nick

turned her around and they walked back up the dirt road onto the paved one.

He seemed to grow more sober, more in control anyway, as they walked. By the time they got to The Hut and had slid into the only free booth among the crowd of high school students, he hardly seemed to need the coffee, but he drank two cups and ate a hamburger, nearly in silence, and brushed off two or three boys who wanted to join them. Not only does everyone know him, Kate thought; they also tolerate whatever he does, as if he couldn't shake their respect even if he wanted to.

"You seem pretty popular," she said hesitantly when they had left and started the long walk back to the car. He didn't touch her now, just walked beside her, keeping space between them.

"What good is it?" he answered with sudden anger. "Tell me that, you-who-know-so-much; what good is it?"

"What do you mean," she asked, "what good is it?"

"See those stars?" He pointed. "If I wanted to be an astronaut, which I did when I was a little kid, if I still wanted to be one, there's no way I could. Know what I'd like? I'd like to go to one of those fancy out-of-sight expensive colleges like your brother's going to, and learn something really terrific, like law maybe, or some kind of science—hell, I don't know."

"Well," began Kate, "then why . . ."

But he interrupted, as if she weren't there.

"Yes, I do know. Got to be practical, right? So I'd get me an MBA and then get a job where some dude would show me all the ropes, you know what I mean? Only there's no way that's going to happen, unless some fancy college wants to pay me to go to it." He laughed bitterly, picking up a pebble he'd kicked and throwing it into the river. After a minute, his voice lower, he went on. "And I'd train in someone else's business for a while and then I'd start my own, and I'd have me a nice wife and a couple of nice kids and we'd live in one of those fancy houses you people have in View, only it'd be *here,* where my folks are, because I love this town, even if it is on the wrong side of the river. Only it's going to be even the wronger side once they get that waste plant in, and that's why not even that part of the dream's any good. You want to make peace between these two towns, baby, you figure out why no one ever told you that one of the sites being considered was in Hastings Bay."

"I—I forgot to ask them the other night, but I'm sure my parents knew all along, I . . ."

"Peacemaker," said Nick, kissing her quickly but with surprising gentleness, "you are something else. I'm going to take you home."

✕⊂ 12

THAT's two kisses, Kate thought lazily, lying in bed the next morning, and neither of them real.

She stretched. What's a real kiss, I wonder. She kissed her pillow lingeringly, then jumped up, feeling self-conscious. I wish I had a sister, she thought, dressing; if I had a sister we could both practice kissing on a pillow and it'd be funny instead of obscene.

The autumn sun poured into the kitchen; the table, now permanently in the middle of the floor, was piled with books, magazines, and newspaper clippings that hadn't been there when she'd gone out last night. Two neat piles of index cards, one written on, the other blank, lay to one side. Kate picked up one of the written-on ones:

"Waste Isolation Power Plant," it said. "New Mexico. 2,600 feet under. Tunnels. Salt strata."

Kate frowned and looked at the next card.

"Love Canal," it said. "Chem., but find out more."

The next—they seemed to be in no particular order —read "Low level: clothes, tools, etc., from reactor crews, medical techs, lab equip. High level: weapons mfr. leavings, unused fuel rods, reactors."

"PLUTONIUM," said the next card in capital letters, "takes more than 24,000 years to lose half its strength."

There was a clumping on the back steps, and Dad came into the kitchen, his hands as grimy as his plaid flannel work shirt, whose rolled-up sleeves exposed equally grimy arms. "Good morning," he said, kissing Kate before going to the sink to wash. "You're up bright and early for a young woman who's been out on the town. How was your date? Is he nice?"

"So-so," said Kate, still looking at the cards; the next few were about radiation-caused cancer. "Did I tell you," she asked, "that I found out when I went to his house for dinner a couple of nights ago that he's got a cute little sister who has leukemia? I told Mom . . ."

Dad turned, soap foaming on his hands. "Yes," he said. "I mean, no, you didn't tell me, but Mom did. That's —but one can't find words for that kind of sadness, can one?"

"No."

Dad sat down, reaching for one of the books.

"Dad, did you know they might put the plant in Hastings Bay instead of here?"

He laid his hand on the book's cover instead of picking it up. "Yes," he said, "but it came as quite a surprise. Looking back, I guess I'd heard references to it before your mother and I went to that meeting, but it never registered before then. I guess everyone assumed I knew, so no one came right out and told me."

"Nick says it'll probably go through," Kate said, "for Hastings, I mean, because Hastings people don't have enough money to fight it."

"That must make him pretty angry." Dad leaned forward. "But, Katy, it's not just money that's needed. In fact, that might be the least of it. It's energy and knowledge and persuasiveness. You can tell your friend Nick that; I'm convinced of it." He patted the pile of books. "Elizabeth Briggs asked me to do a piece for the paper, a sort of informational piece, as a start. That's why I have all this stuff." He looked thoughtful. "Maybe I could talk to the Browns. I've been thinking anyway that if Hastings Bay's a possible site, too, the two towns should be joining forces."

Kate went to the refrigerator and poured herself and her father some juice. "Do you really think everyone would work together?" she asked uncertainly, remembering Nick's vehemence the night before.

"I'm not sure. But maybe. You say the kids don't get along, but that doesn't mean the adults couldn't." He took the glass of juice she handed him. "Thanks. You work on the kids and I'll work on the adults, okay? That way we ought to be able to conquer the world—at least these two towns, anyway."

It turned into a quiet end-of-summer day, already too hot after breakfast to run. Besides, she'd have to run alone; Pippa was going to be out with Vinnie all day until she had to go home to help entertain some relatives at dinner. Maybe tonight when it cools off, Kate thought lazily, I'll run by myself.

She did a couple of hours' worth of homework, read some of the paper, and then went outside and helped her father fence in a corner of the backyard for the compost he planned to make when the leaves fell. She made a chocolate pudding for dessert and afterward peered into Dan's room to see if he was free, but he was at his desk and nice-bearishly growled, "Busy—sorry." Finally, she took her latest library book to the backyard, set up a lawn chair, and read.

Or tried to read; the book was good, but her mind kept wandering, sometimes into the blankness caused by the unseasonably warm weather and the clear blueness of the sky, and sometimes to Nick, then Jon, then Nick again, then Pippa. *I hardly remember,* she realized, *what Chelsea looks like.* Funny, she thought for the second time in the last couple of weeks, how things change. How people change.

Could I marry a person like Nick, she wondered, giving up on the book and turning it facedown in her lap. *Or Jon?* She tried to visualize herself as someone's wife, someone's mother, as Pippa visualized herself, making breakfast and seeing everyone off. She pictured Pippa in an apron, waving at a shadowy husband and kids, one of whom looked like Cassie. But the scene didn't work when she built it around herself, not in the same way, anyhow. She could see herself with Jon, maybe, living in a tiny apartment in a nameless city. Of course she didn't even like cities, but she and Jon wouldn't stay for long. Besides, it would be a real city, a big one, not a small complacent one like Providence—New York, maybe, or even Paris. Maybe she'd write some poems good enough to read aloud at one of those bookstore parties where there were specially invited guests, wine, and literary conversation. She could imagine Jon standing in the back, watching her proudly, then perhaps playing his guitar for the audience while she watched . . .

What was that line he'd sung to her? Something about "silvergirl"? It sounded vaguely familiar but she couldn't place where it was from. It was comfortably unlike her old nickname, though, and another Jon had given her, joking, long ago: "Plain Kate, and bonny Kate, and sometimes Kate the curst." That was from Shakespeare, *The Taming of the Shrew;* they'd stayed up to see it on TV one fall night in sixth grade.

"Kate!" Dan called from the house. "Telephone."

"I was just thinking of you," she said about twenty minutes later as she and Jon biked toward the river, "when you called."

He smiled but didn't answer, and she pedaled silently beside him in the still heat. He turned off at the side of the bridge and they pushed the bikes through the brush to their old frogging place, more open now that a few of summer's leaves had fallen, but still hidden from the road. The surrounding bushes were so high and thick they would conceal the little pond even when they were leafless.

The warm, late-afternoon sun beamed lazily onto the quiet water, smoothing it with light.

Jon sat down, leaning against a mossy rock they'd put their frogging buckets on spring after spring. "How was your date?" he asked, patting the ground beside him.

So that's it, Kate thought, sitting down; he's jealous.

"Okay," she said. "Nick drinks a lot. He got drunk. But just when you think he's going to—try something, he gets okay again. Maybe he wasn't as drunk as he seemed."

"Did he?" asked Jon, pulling up a tuft of grass and shredding it methodically. "I mean did he try anything?"

"Well," said Kate, teasing him a little, "he did kiss me."

"And I suppose you liked it."

"It wasn't much of a kiss," she said. "But yes, I guess it was nice."

Without warning Jon pulled her roughly to him and kissed her, hard, not gently as Nick had. She was so surprised she couldn't kiss back, could only let her mouth be flattened under his.

"Ouch!" she protested when he released her. "That hurt!"

"I'm sorry," he said. "Katy, I—I'm sorry." He took her hand and leaned toward her, kissing her softly, carefully, till she moved into his arms to kiss him back and her head swam and her heart began to pound. "Jon," she heard herself say when he pulled back a little—but he still held her, kissing her neck, moving his hand gently on her back. "Jon."

He stopped, his hands on her shoulders. "I just don't want you to think I don't want to do that, Miss Kettle," he said. "I just don't want you to think I don't know how."

She didn't know what to say, or what she felt, except dizziness. There I was this morning, she was thinking, practicing on my pillow, and here I am now, doing the real thing. Oh, lord, is this what growing up is going to be like?

"You—you do seem to know how, Mr. Pot," she said shakily.

He took her hand again. "Katy," he said. "Katy." He smiled ruefully. "I don't know much about this," he admitted. "I'm sure Nick knows a lot more. I'm sure Nick's slept with girls. I haven't. But, Katy, if I did, I'd want it to be you."

Kate felt herself grow more light-headed; something seemed stuck in her throat. At last she said, "I'm not sure how I feel about that, Jon."

"About me?" he asked. "Or about the whole thing in general? Sex." He said it very clearly, as if for the first time.

"Both, really." Then, seeing his crestfallen look, Kate touched his hand, saying, "Oh, no, I don't mean it like that! I do know how I feel about you. I—I love you, Jon, more than I love anyone . . ."

Before she could go on, relief flooded his eyes, and he whispered, "Me, too. I love you, too, Katy. I always have. You're . . ."

"But—but I'm not sure *how* I love you. Not how much," she added hastily. "Just how. We're so—so close, we know each other so well; we're so much alike. I'm not sure if we—you know. It—" She felt embarrassed, then told herself it was Jon, for Pete's sake, and said, "I'm not sure about, you know, sleeping together. Just yet, anyway."

Jon laughed. "Thank God," he said, throwing back his head. "I'm not either. Only I know I'd do it if you wanted. I'd do just about anything you wanted."

"You shouldn't, Jon," she said seriously. "You shouldn't do anything you don't want to do, not for me."

"But I would, you know. I really would." He picked a blade of grass, stretched it between his thumbs, and blew, making a horrible mooselike noise. Kate clapped her hands over her ears, laughing.

"I was so jealous," he said, taking her hands down, looking into her eyes. "I kept thinking of him—*with* you —and I couldn't sleep all last night and I was so mad all day I couldn't call you—till I did call you." He took her hands again. "Katy, I just want you to know I'd . . . Of course," he said, abruptly dropping her hands, "maybe you have already, and . . ." He turned away, reddening.

"No." She tried not to smile. "No, I haven't."

"Well," he said, looking at her again, "we're even, then, I guess."

She wondered suddenly how he felt about girls in general, and if he felt more for boys, but sitting there with him, watching him, she thought, no, Jon doesn't feel that way about anyone yet, just as I don't—no, not just as I don't; with me it's not feeling ready, but with him it's different somehow.

"Penny?" asked Jon.

"Oh, don't, Mr. Pot, please."

"Okay." He stood up, holding out his hand, and pulled her to her feet. "The worst thing about growing up, maybe, is beginning to have secret thoughts."

She hugged him quickly. "No thought I have can ever be secret from you for long, you know that." She wondered if that was true. "It's just not the right time for this one. Okay?"

He bent swiftly and kissed her again, on the cheek, lightly, and they biked home as the sun, its heat diminishing, began spilling its gold into the downstream end of the river.

13

"WHAT WE NEED is a plan," said Kate.

"What we need," said Pippa, "is a party." She bent and loosened the laces on her running shoes, then took them off, holding her legs out from the River Road stone wall they were sitting on, and wiggling her toes. "Well, why not?"

Kate looked at her. "With kids from both sides," she said slowly, "kids who aren't really involved. Maybe several parties—so word will spread and eventually the others will see it's okay to be friends."

"We could have the first one around Halloween, maybe. You know, so we could give it a theme or something." Pippa swung her legs up on the wall and faced Kate. "Halloween's too far away, though," she said. "Maybe we'd better have it before then."

"Pippa?" Kate looked out over the field that spread below them, rolling into hills and then woods, with horses quietly grazing. "Do you think it'd work? I mean, do you think anyone would come?"

Pippa stretched, throwing back her shoulders. "People like parties," she said. "They ought to come."

"Should we tell them right away that kids from the other side will be coming? Or—or should we be sneaky? You could invite the Hastings kids and I could invite the View ones."

Pippa shook her head emphatically. "Word'll get around anyway, and people will be mad if we're sneaky about it." She jumped off the wall. "Nope. Let's call a spade a spade, like my dad says. Where should we have it?"

"We could have it at my house, I guess," Kate said. "I'd have to ask Mom, but I think she'd say it was okay." And, she thought, maybe I can talk Dan into being home that night, just in case. If he's willing, after what happened to him . . .

"Will that be all right?" Pippa was asking. "I'd say my place, but Cassie's got to go into Children's Hospital for some treatments pretty soon, and . . ."

Impulsively, Kate touched Pippa's arm. "Oh, Pip," she said, "you're always so brave, I forget about Cassie. I'm sorry. Are the treatments very awful?"

"No, not really. Mostly just an intravenous thing. We take turns reading to her, keeping her quiet. She misses her cat, though, and this time she'll miss the kittens. I wish . . ." She stopped.

"What?" Kate asked gently.

"Oh," said Pippa, "that I could have leukemia for her." She shook her head, tears glistening on her lashes. "Like every month when I'm writhing with cramps, Mom says she wishes she could have them for me. But she can't, and I can't make Cassie better by being sick myself, and I guess that's what life's like. Most of the time you can't help the people you love even if what happens to them isn't fair."

"I know," said Kate, thinking of her father and, for some reason she couldn't fathom, of Jon. "I know."

Pippa looked toward the horses, one of whom was now

nuzzling another's neck. "Cassie has a fifty-percent chance of recovery. Only some days, when she's tired and cranky and we know she feels rotten, I realize that also means a fifty-percent chance of dying." She turned back to Kate. "It's awful, Kate, for someone so little to be so sick! That whole hospital, it's full of kids like her, lots of them dying. Last time Cassie was in there, there was this little girl named Lisa in the next bed, about nine years old but so thin she was just about all head. She had this big smile and beautiful eyes, always friendly and cheerful. One day we were there early because Cassie had to have some awful test, and while we were waiting Lisa woke up and said, 'I just love first thing in the morning because everything's new and maybe it'll be a *good* day.' She said it like that, emphasizing the 'good,' and she said she hoped the rest of the day would be good for Cassie, even though the beginning wasn't. And then she died that afternoon, without ever seeing another fresh, hopeful morning. From then on I've been sure that no matter how much we pray, some night, or some beautiful new morning, Cassie'll die, too . . ." Pippa's voice broke.

Kate jumped down off the wall and put her arms around Pippa, turning her to face her, smoothing her hair, rubbing her back, cradling Pippa's head as if she were a small child. She wanted desperately to say something but no words came and she stood there helplessly till Pippa's sobs lessened, trying to let her hands speak for her.

Pippa patted Kate's shoulder, then moved away slightly. "Damn. I never have a Kleenex."

Kate groped at the waistband of her shorts and pulled one out. "It's a little sweaty," she said, "but unused."

"Thanks," Pippa said. "I'm sorry."

"Don't be."

"I haven't cried about Cassie for a long time. I don't dare, at home. We all try to act normal, pretend nothing's wrong, for her sake, but for our own, too." Pippa sniffed. "Hey, listen," she said, "it's going to be a great party; I feel it in my bones, you know what I mean? And it's going to work, and it'll have been your idea . . ."

"*Your* idea."

"Well, maybe a little bit. But you're the one who started thinking about the whole problem." Pippa grinned. "Nick doesn't call you Peacemaker for nothing."

Kate grimaced; Pippa gave her arm a playful punch, and then retrieved her shoes. "Okay if Vinnie comes?" she asked, putting them on. "Even though he's out of school and all?"

"Sure, why not?"

"I mean, he is kind of friends with Nick," Pippa said chattily. "Of course he used to be kind of involved in the feud and all, but since he's been out of school he's been out of touch with it, at least mostly. He said just the other day he thinks it's kind of silly . . ."

"Pippa," Kate laughed. "It's okay!"

They decided to have the party that coming weekend, for the weekend after that was the first big at-home football game, and on the next one the sophomores were putting on a carnival to raise money for their class trip. Kate's mother, after some initial panic about housecleaning and still-full book cartons, enthusiastically worked out a shopping list with Kate and Pippa, and Kate and Pippa, with a good deal of trepidation, began deciding whom to invite.

Jon, of course, and Carol Lodge and Marcia Brooks, and Ricky Jarvis and Charlie Moss, along with most of the others who'd been at the pond the night Dan was hurt. Not Rab, though, or Karen Anderson, or anyone else who was clearly trying to keep the feud alive.

Pippa came up with a similarly neutral group from Hastings, including Vinnie—not Nick, not Skid. "Nick'll be mad, maybe," she said, "but I think he'll understand. And this way there'll be no one coming who might get into a fight. It should be fine."

At first, it was. By half past nine on the night of the party, about thirty people were dancing in Kate's living room, or sitting around in groups eating and talking. Dan, who had agreed without hesitation to play bouncer if necessary ("My chance for revenge," he'd said wryly), drifted in and out but eventually, with a nod to Kate, went upstairs to join their parents, who were watching TV in their bedroom. Kate moved from group to group, trying to spend extra time with those from Hastings Bay, and she saw Pippa concentrating on View people, usually with Vinnie, a solid, surprisingly unattractive presence at her side. If you described his face feature by feature, Kate decided when she met him, it would sound awful. His nose was large and hooked; one of his front teeth was broken at an angle; and the flesh of his face was pitted, as if he had had terrible acne not long before. But when he smiled at her she felt bathed in sunlight, and instantly she understood why Pippa liked him in spite of wanting to date someone "less like everyone else." Besides, he had the deepest, mellowest voice she'd ever heard.

"Hi, Peacemaker," Vinnie greeted her later in the evening when he and Pippa ended up in the kitchen with Kate getting potato chip refills. He smiled, adding, "Jon Westgate's got good taste."

Kate felt herself blushing. "How do you think it's going?" she asked, pouring chips into bowls to cover her embarrassment. She handed Vinnie one bowl and picked up another herself. "Do you think everyone's mixing okay?"

"Well," he said, opening the door to the living room for her and Pippa, "I saw at least one Hastings kid dancing with a River View kid. See?" He nodded toward a couple who were laughing as they danced. "Looks like they're still at it. Hey, Tanner," he shouted after looking appreciatively at the girl who, Kate saw, was Carol Lodge, "you're crossin' the river in style, huh?"

The boy winked and gave Vinnie a thumbs-up sign.

Just as he did, Kate felt a blast of air from the hall, and a moment later, Rab plus several of his followers elbowed their way into the living room. "But isn't this the place?" Rab said, mock-bewildered, into the thick silence that greeted him, incongruously backed by drums and guitars and a whining vocalist from the tape that was still playing. "Ah, yes—Katy, Vin—it must be. The peacemaking party, right?" He hunched his shoulders elegantly, palms up. "As I told my friends here"— he indicated the shuffling chorus behind him—"one party's as good as another." He reached into his pocket and pulled out a bottle of bourbon; a few people looked alarmed, but one or two—from River View, Kate noticed—cheered.

"Rab."

Kate saw Jon detach himself from the wall he'd been leaning against and go up to him.

"Rab," Jon said quietly, "the bottle's out of place, man, and so are you. And your friends . . ."

"Oh, yeah, wimp?" Rab took a swig from the bottle and handed it to a snickering boy behind him. "Tell me about it." He swaggered to the fireplace and draped himself against the mantel. "You guys'll be glad enough we're here in a few minutes," he said, raising his voice above the music.

"How come?" Jon asked coldly, following him.

"Because, wimp, Skid and Nick and company are on their way over. 'S why I came—I mean, even if this party's a juvenile idea, it *is* on our side, and if there's going to be an invasion, you guys'll need some protection, you know?" He left the fireplace and put an arm around Kate, who had moved closer, trying to think of something to say. "Especially our hostess, here."

There was a commotion at the door, and loud voices, and Kate's heart sank. She wriggled away from Rab and went to the door to find that Dan had come downstairs, probably drawn by the noise of Rab's entrance, and was holding the door half open, shaking his head firmly at Skid, who stood there grinning. Nick and several other boys stood behind him in the dim porch light. " 'Fraid not, fellas," Dan was saying, "another time, maybe, but this is a small party."

Vinnie moved away from Pippa and confronted Skid. "Wrong house," he said abruptly, poking his chin toward Dan. "Nick, you jerk, can't you get Skid out of here?"

Kate moved decisively between them, pasting a smile on her face that must, she told herself ironically, look as phony as Rab's. She managed a brief, more sincere one at Nick as she reached for his hand. "Come on in," she said, with as much friendliness as she could muster. "You might as well, since you're here." She held the door open, ignoring Dan's protests. Skid, with a defiant toss of his head, shouldered his way in, passing Rab as indifferently as if he were air.

Dan, his face strained, put his hand on Kate's arm. "Kate, that's . . ."

"Later," she whispered to him. "It's all right. At least I think it is. Just—just stick around, okay?"

"Kate . . ." she heard him say, but the tape in the living room ended and there was an even thicker silence than before. She patted Dan's hand and went in, trying to ignore the cold stares between Rab's crew and Skid's as she reached for another tape and said in a voice that sounded too high, "What's the matter? No one's dancing!" What a dumb thing to say, she thought, trying to hide how she felt, and as the music started she danced toward Skid, nudging Pippa purposefully on the way. She danced around him; Skid watched, not moving, till Pippa put her hand on Rab's shoulder and Carol went up to Nick. As soon as Nick started dancing, Skid did also, and after a while, he even seemed genuinely friendly. Out of the corner of her eye, Kate saw Rab bend closer to Pippa and laugh at something she said. Soon afterward, though, he snickered loudly at a comment from one of his henchmen and, breaking away from Pippa and hurling something pointed about "children" in Skid's direction, he left.

By that time, Hastings Bay groups and River View groups were mingling in earnest, ignoring the crashers, talking with each other, dancing . . .

"Not just one or two either," Kate said, bursting jubilantly into her parents' room later when everyone had gone home, "but all of them, some of the worst ones, even, at least for a while, and there was no fighting, even when Rab was still there along with Skid and Nick . . ." She looked around then; her parents and Dan, whom she now saw sitting on a chair in the corner, were oddly silent. "What's the matter?" she asked. "Too much noise? What?"

"Katy," said her father, "Dan thinks he recognized those boys from Hastings Bay who crashed. He thinks they're the ones who beat him up."

Kate stared at her father, then at Dan.

"The one you called Skid?" Dan said. "Him. And a couple of the others with him."

"Oh, God," said Kate, going to him, her mouth dry and coppery-tasting. Of course, it had to be—but Skid had seemed so friendly when he'd danced with her! "Oh, Danny, I'm sorry!" She hesitated, not wanting to seem crass—but I have to know, she told herself. "Not—not Nick?" she asked nervously. "Do you remember the one named Nick?"

"I don't think he was one of them," Dan said.

Kate hugged him, but part of her, she knew, was rejoicing. At least it wasn't Nick, she thought; not the leader, not—the words popped unbidden into her mind —not my friend.

By Monday morning when she walked into school, Kate still hadn't decided how to react to Skid. Part of her wanted to confront him angrily for daring to come to the house of someone he'd beaten up, but another part wanted to believe that he hadn't known or that he'd come in a clumsy, indirect attempt to make amends. Either way, she thought, I can't risk whatever good thing's started—so she said hello as cheerfully as she could when she saw him in the hall with Nick.

"Hi," he said back, noncommittally. "Nice party."

She spent the rest of the morning feeling disloyal to her brother.

That afternoon, there was a special assembly, at which a public relations man from the United American Waste Disposal Company spoke for an hour and a half, after explaining that his company was the one that had been hired by the state to build "an experimental nuclear waste dumping and processing plant" in River View (Site One) or Hastings Bay (Site Two). The plant's customers, he said, would be the state and possibly also the federal government, as well as private industry under contract to the government. The latest disposal and processing techniques would be used. It would be quite safe, he said, and the lucky community in which the plant was eventually located would benefit enormously, both because there would be more jobs for its citizens and because "the eyes of the nation will be upon you, and you will be pioneering, making a tremendous contribution to one of the most pressing problems of our time: how to dispose—*safely*—of nuclear waste in the heavily populated Northeast. We've already tested our methods as much as we can in laboratory conditions. Now it's time to do the real thing in the real world."

During the question period that followed, a few people asked about jobs at the plant—seniors, mostly, and a couple of people who, Kate knew, had unemployed fathers or older brothers. Then Charlie Moss raised his hand and asked, hostility barely hidden, "Are you gentlemen at United American aware that Hastings Bay and River View are just what their names sound like—on a river?"

"The waste," said the public relations man coldly, "will not come in contact with the river."

"Even when it floods in the spring?" Skid called out. "Man, last spring this school was full of water. You couldn't go down to the basement without a boat. They had to put in all new lockers."

The man's voice became colder as he said, "The waste will not touch the water. And"—he held up his hand —"it will not seep into the ground. We will build pits lined with clay and the newest plastics; we will use drums made of material stronger and more permanent than steel."

"Will they last 24,000 years?" Kate heard herself asking, one of her father's index cards floating into her memory. "My dad says plutonium takes longer than that to finish breaking down. That's a big ingredient in nuclear things, isn't it?"

"That's one of the points of our experimental plant,"

the man said—uncomfortably, Kate saw with satisfaction, "to test certain materials . . ."

"What if your tests fail?" Jon interrupted. "I mean, you're disposing of bombs, right? What if one of them goes off before it's disarmed? And if you're testing storage drums, some materials are bound to be better than others."

"We will take all possible precautions," the man said, looking at the principal as if for help. "All possible precautions . . ."

"Will you take precautions," Pippa asked, her voice shaking, "against radiation leaks and things like that? My little sister has leukemia—not from any kind of waste dump. But I know radiation can give people cancer. And I wouldn't want anyone to go through what my sister's going through. She's only four years old."

The man spread his hands in apparent defeat. "Look, I know it's hard to trust a stranger," he said. "And you're right to be concerned. But remember, the government's going to be supervising all this very carefully, and so is our company. We're not new at this; we've also experimented in the Southwest with underground caves, and off the West Coast with sea disposal. Kids, remember this: every year we have a greater need for efficient disposal, for every year we need more and more nuclear power, more and more weapons, more and more nuclear medicine."

"To cure the diseases that you cause," Pippa said, her voice steady now, with anger. "Right?"

"Nuclear energy," said the man, "nuclear power, nuclear medicine—they're lifesavers, not destroyers. Ask your science teachers, kids; in fact, as I understand it, you're going to be having some special, er, lessons in all that for the next couple of weeks, to help you understand . . ."

Someone shouted "Boo!" and several people hissed. In another second the auditorium was ringing with jeers and the principal and two assistant principals were standing on the stage in front of the frightened public relations man, holding up their hands for silence. Someone—Kate never knew who—blew a gym whistle, and for a moment there was a surprised pause while everyone looked around to see who had done it.

"People," shouted the principal, "people. I am ashamed of you! This is a democratic society and a democratic school. We invited this gentleman here to give us all information—the same information your parents have been receiving in mailings and meetings and in the papers, which, let's face it, not all of us have read as diligently as we might. Your parents are going to register their opinions by voting on this proposal at special town meetings in both Hastings Bay and River View in a few weeks; we thought some of you might want to have enough background so you can voice *your* opinions at those meetings."

"Why should we?" someone shouted. "We can't vote."

"Look, not even your parents' votes will be binding," said the principal, "but their votes will send a message to Boston and Washington about how people here feel about the issue. Your opinions could influence that message, maybe even contribute to it actively."

"They'll just take the land anyway, the way I hear it," someone shouted—Ricky Jarvis, Kate saw, turning around. "Whichever place they want."

"It'll be Hastings Bay," someone else said. "Who cares about Hastings? River View'll bribe some politician and . . ."

"It'll be in View," another voice called out. "The site's better."

"People, people," said the principal again. "Let's work together on this, like reasonable human beings. After all, as our guest said, some community has to have this plant. That's the point—to see how it works in a crowded area."

"Why?" came a shout from the back. "Why not put it away from where people live?"

"Away from water . . ."

"Away from the world."

There was a laugh, and a momentary calm after the relief it brought.

During the lull, Kate stood up nervously. "If we don't like it," she said, "if both towns don't like it, both sets of kids, both sets of parents, that's a start, isn't it? A kind of agreement. Why can't we work together to fight it? There was a party at my house the other night . . ."

But everyone was talking at once now, angrily, and suddenly she saw the party for what it must have been despite the good part at the end: a curiosity, nothing more.

Nick's voice rose above the others: ". . . make up their minds to do something, those politicians, you can bet they're going to try every trick they know to do it, no matter what anyone else thinks. It's everyone for himself now, if anyone's going to come out ahead."

Later, he stopped Kate in the hall. "Your party was fun," he said, "and I'm glad I crashed it. I see what you're trying to do. But like they say, the party's over. This is serious business now. It's us or you—Hastings Bay or River View. How can we get together on a thing like that? Tell me that, Peacemaker. Tell me that."

14

"They didn't even listen," Kate said to her parents and brother furiously that night at dinner. "They didn't even listen. Everyone was talking at once, and Nick was the loudest—*Nick*, after coming to the party and everything. I thought that meant something, his coming, even if he did crash, and Rab's coming, and the fact that kids from both sides danced together and talked. And that Skid came, even—I'm sorry, Dan. But now it's all as if it never happened, as if Nick didn't really notice, even if he did say something about knowing what I was trying to do."

Kate saw her parents exchange a look and, as her fury subsided into near tears, her mother covered her hand with her own and said, "As you told us your friend Nick said, Katy, the party's over. There are some things you can't solve that way. And, honey, it was *terrible* of those boys to come, the ones who hurt Dan. I can't believe they came for any good reason. If your father and I had known . . ."

"You're doing it, too," Kate said, turning an anguished face to her. "You're doing it, too, just keeping the same old fight going. How can you? You—you're more of a peacemaker than I am, how can you just want to—to do the same thing back?"

"She's right, Julie," Dad said softly. "You see how

hard it is to be fair when someone you love is threat-
ened."

"Yes, it's hard," said Mom. "I'm learning every day
just how hard it is." She turned to Kate. "Maybe it's not
possible to be a one-hundred-percent pacifist. Maybe it's
not even right."

Kate stared at her. "I don't believe this," she said when
she could speak, close to tears again. "I just plain don't
believe it. You, of all people, when you've always . . . It's
—it's like you're a traitor, a . . ."

"Kate!" admonished her father sharply.

Kate's mother's lips pulled tightly together for a moment, then relaxed as if with an effort. "That's a strong
word, Kate," she said quietly. "Maybe you'd better think
of it in relation to yourself and your brother."

"Hey . . ." Dan began—but Kate barely heard him. She
felt the hot tears ready to spill over and, muttering, "Excuse me," she fled to her room.

Am I a traitor to Dan, she asked herself miserably
when her sobs finally began to die away. Am I?

Is family more important than the world, the whole
town?

"It can't be," she moaned into her wet pillow. "Even
if you want it to be, how can it be?"

She thought of an argument they'd had around the
dinner table a couple of years back, when Dad had been
telling about the fallout shelters people had built in the
fifties and sixties, because of the chance of nuclear war.
Some people, he'd said, wanted to keep guns in their
shelters to turn away outsiders, to shoot them, even. He
and Dan had both said they'd consider doing that, to
preserve the family. Kate and her mother had been ap-

palled. "What would be the good of living in a world like that?" Mom had said. "A world in which people cared only about themselves?"

What would you say now, Mom, Kate wondered bitterly.

But, she thought, rolling over onto her back, I can't change my mind the way she did. I can't. I just can't. Not because I don't love Dan, but because he's only one person.

There was a knock at her door and then Pippa's voice said uncertainly, "Kate? May I come in?"

Kate sat up, startled, pushing her pillow away. "Sure," she said, stammering the word, repeating it, then running her fingers through her tangled hair. Had the doorbell rung?

Pippa pushed the door open, and, looking as if she didn't know whether to expect someone who was hysterical or just morose, came over to Kate. "Your mom said you were up here," she explained. "She said you'd probably tell me to go away if you didn't want to see me." Pippa dug into her pocket. "Here," she said, handing Kate a tissue. "One good turn deserves another."

"Thanks." Kate blew her nose. "I must look awful. Here, sit down." She scrunched toward the wall, making room for Pippa on the bed.

"I come with an apology," Pippa said, sitting. "Nick's. We joked a lot about wrapping it up in white paper and tying it with a pink ribbon. I told him I thought you'd like blue or green better but he insisted on pink. So pretend it's pink. Now where did I put it?" She pretended to rummage through her pockets, then looked up anxiously. "No laugh, huh? Okay. I guess it's not a laughing matter, is it?"

Tears rose in Kate's eyes and, not trusting her voice, she shook her head.

"Nick says he's sorry he was one of the people who interrupted you at assembly. He said he's sorry for what he said afterward, too, and he wants to know if you'll go with him to the movies tonight, or if you'll go with him Saturday to Green Lake. He said to tell you he knows it's too cold to swim, but he's pretty good with oars."

Anger against Nick filled her again and she turned away, stopping Pippa midsentence. Why did Nick think he could say anything in the world to her and get away with it? Why did he think he could hurt her feelings one minute and the next find her ready to laugh with him, go out with him as if nothing had happened? Why didn't he take her seriously? That was it; he didn't. Probably none of them did.

But why should they? She certainly wasn't making any progress.

"No thanks," she said stiffly. "Please tell Nick I'd rather not."

"Kate," Pippa said, "please. Listen. Nick also said to tell you that there isn't time for peacemaking now, that things have gone too far for that. That it's not just a kids' fight anymore, but a matter of life and death . . ."

"If it weren't for the kids' fight," Kate retorted, "then maybe the kids could do something about the life-and-death one. There's always got to be time to make peace." She stopped, knowing that she sounded like her mother in the old days. For the first time it seemed a bit pompous, but she shook off the thought, reasoning that the idea was more important than the way presenting it made her sound, and that if she started worrying about what people thought of her, she might easily waver again. Dan was right, though, she realized; it's *not* a popular idea.

"Tell Nick," she said aloud, feeling her confidence grow with the strength of her convictions, and trying to push her feelings under, "that the reason why it's important to go on with the peacemaking is that it *is* a matter of life and death. That's exactly why we can't stop."

But Pippa looked unconvinced. "Mom took Cassie to the hospital this morning. That's sooner than she was supposed to go. She's been feeling sick for the last few days, and this morning she could hardly get out of bed. The doctor said to take her right in. Her remission's probably over, he said. Radiation *does* cause cancer, Kate; that's been proved. I don't want there to be any more Cassies."

Kate took Pippa's hand. "Oh, Pip, I'm sorry," she said. "I truly am." She hesitated, then couldn't help adding, "But don't you see? It's *because* of that, because there could be more Cassies that we have to work together."

"Nick says we have to take care of our own," said Pippa, standing up shakily, "and I think maybe he's right. No one will look after the Browns but the Browns, and no one will look after Hastings Bay but Hastings Bay."

"And you?" Kate asked, feeling as if she were the only person left in the world. "What do you say?"

"I'm torn, Kate. You both make sense to me. I don't want the feud to go on, and I don't want either town to have the waste plant. But I suppose if it has to be in one town or the other, and I have to make a choice, I'll choose River View. I'd choose to keep it out of my town, away from my family." She looked at Kate. "Wouldn't you? If you were really honest about it, wouldn't you, too?"

Before Kate could answer, Pippa left.

By midweek, things gradually improved between Kate and her mother, as if neither of them wanted to acknowledge the new gulf between them. But the tension around school was so thick Kate felt she could almost see it. Scuffles broke out in the cafeteria almost every day, over trivial things, and quickly grew bitter, occasionally brutal. Someone from River View accused someone from Hastings Bay of cheating; someone from Hastings Bay accused someone from River View of siphoning gas from his car. Kate and Pippa avoided each other at the beginning of the week, two strangers sharing a locker, but on Wednesday morning, Pippa left a note for Kate saying, "Hey, Peacemaker, I have no war with you, no matter what I might think of what you think," and by that afternoon they were, tentatively, friends again. Nick, however, still seemed to be avoiding Kate and she certainly didn't go out of her way to see him. Skid also ignored her, as if following Nick's lead, which, she realized, he usually did; maybe that's why he seemed so nice at the party. And Rab wouldn't talk to her, not even to answer when she said hi to him in the hall.

It didn't help that town meeting was only a little more than three weeks away on both sides of the river. A rash of bumper stickers appeared, green for View, blue for Bay, saying (View) PLANTS ARE FOR GARDENS, VOTE NO and

(Bay) SAVE OUR KIDS, DUMP THE WASTE DUMP. View cars were given angry stares as they passed through Hastings Bay; bonfires were lit every night on the Hastings boat launch, not just on weekends. The River View police increased their patrols near the bridge and stopped any car with teenagers in it. If they were from Hastings, they were turned back unless they could give a verifiable address as a destination.

"Tomorrow," said Jon, his hands on Kate's shoulders as they stood in the Ice Cream Shack's line after school on Friday, "we are going to get out of here. We're going to drive to New Hampshire, just you and me. I bet you haven't climbed Monadnock since you were a little kid, right?"

"I—no, actually, I don't remember ever climbing it. Dan was going to, before Harvard started, but I don't think he did."

"Dan's not coming," said Jon. "Just you and me." He studied her running shoes. "You could do it in those," he said, "although boots would be better. But we won't go on the hard trails anyway, since you're out of practice."

"Out of practice!" Kate said, laughing for the first time in days. "I haven't climbed anything steeper than stairs or a tree in my whole life. Maybe Mom has some boots; she used to hike with Dad." Will I ask her, though, she wondered.

Later that afternoon she did, and her mother eagerly presented her with a pair of well-worn boots. She watched anxiously while Kate tried them on, as if it would be a sign of forgiveness if they fit.

They were a little small.

"Better not risk blisters," Mom said, tossing them back

in her closet. After a moment, she turned around decisively. "Kate," she began. "I think you and I . . ."

"It's okay," said Kate quickly, not wanting to discuss it. But her mother held out her hand to her, and pulled her to the side of the bed, sitting her down the way she'd done when Kate was little and needed a serious talk. "Katy," she said, "can we start with the fact that I'm your friend?"

"You're also my mother," Kate said, and then wanted to take it back, for it sounded harsher than she felt. But she couldn't, so she went on. "You're the one I've always looked up to."

"And now," said her mother slowly, "you can't because we don't agree?"

Put that way, it sounded a lot simpler than it felt, even a little silly. "I—no," said Kate. "Not just that. I—"

"You're trying to do something very difficult," said Mom, sitting down beside her. "And I admire you for it. But you're so caught up in it, you're forgetting something else very important—people. I don't think," she said more softly, "that you're really a traitor to Dan or to anyone. I was upset, too. I want to go on being a pacifist, Kate, but it's hard sometimes, that's all. It's been hard before, and I've weathered it. I'm sure I will this time, too. Every pacifist has to learn it's not always easy or uncomplicated." She put her hand under Kate's chin and looked into her eyes. "Okay?"

Kate managed a nod.

"I'm sorry I called you a traitor," said Mom.

"I—I sort of called you one, too, didn't I?"

"Sort of." Her mother stood up. "Okay if neither of us is?"

Kate felt herself smiling. "Okay," she said.

"Good. Now—" Mom leaned down and examined Kate's running shoes, picking up one and then the other, peering at the soles. "These look pretty good, actually. Thank goodness you have strong ankles. Let's see what Dan thinks, though. And what about a knapsack? You might want to take lunch."

Both Dad and Dan, consulted after dinner, thought the running shoes would do fine, if she was careful. "It's not that tough a mountain," Dan said. And yes, he had a small day pack she could borrow, and Dad had an old canteen. "Oranges," said Mom. "You'll want oranges."

"Better take my knife," said Dan, handing over his Swiss Army one.

"And a bandana," said her mother, turning toward the hall closet. "It'll do in a pinch for a triangular bandage."

"Dan," said Dad, twinkling, "just run down to the cellar, would you, and bring up my old ice ax and the newer crampons."

"And," Mom said, laughing, "that rope you used in the Himalayas. Okay, so you're not climbing Everest." She hugged Kate, quickly, just barely giving Kate time to hug back. "But it does pay to be careful, since you haven't exactly grown up scaling great heights."

"I wish I were coming with you," said Dad wistfully. "Monadnock may be little but it's beautiful—one of my favorite places in the world."

"You wait till spring, Jim," said Mom, "and see what the doctor says. Maybe then we could go, maybe even climb some other little mountains, too. Now Kate," she said, turning to her, "about lunch . . ."

"Oh, Family," said Kate, throwing her arms around all of them at once as nearly as she could, relieved to be feeling friends with her mother again, "I love you!"

15

THE NEXT DAY was beautiful, crisp and clear, with a sharp
edge to the air but not enough of one to make it uncomfortably cold. "But remember," Jon warned, as they
crossed the river and turned north, "it'll be a lot colder
on top—windy, too. Have you got a warm shirt and
stuff?"

Kate laughed. "I have got," she said, "enough gear for
a week's backpacking."

He looked critically at her pack. "You sure that's not
too much?"

"I don't think so," she said. "It's really not heavy at all,
but it does move around a bit more than I'd like."

"We'll repack it there. Didn't know I was an expert,
did you?"

"No," she said. "But then I guess there might still be
a few things about you that I have to catch up on. Four
years is a long time."

"True." Jon carefully negotiated the turn onto the
highway that would take them to New Hampshire. "But
you know all the important things about me." He patted
her knee. "Today," he said, "there is no feud, no waste
plant, no Rab or Skid or Nick or even Pippa. You and
I are going to rediscover the world. Agreed?"

Kate sat back in her seat. "Agreed," she said.

．　．　．

They got there in just under two hours. A few minutes later, after Jon had deftly rearranged Kate's pack and swapped a few of the things in his for some from hers in order to distribute weight and shapes more easily, they set out, Jon with a well-used trail map in his back pocket. "All we need," he said cheerfully as they started up a swiftly rising path, "is a good dog. There's nothing like a dog for climbing mountains like this one." He smiled, but seemed focused on something inside himself. "Whenever I went hiking with Hank's family, we took his dog, and she was wonderful, nosing into everything, making discoveries. She walked two or three times as far as we did because she kept running ahead and then coming back to tell us what she'd found."

"Did you do a lot of things with Hank?" Kate asked curiously.

He turned to face her. "Yes," he said simply, "I did. And I miss him a lot. You'd have liked him—you will like him. I'll point him out to you sometime. He's still around but he's changed schools. We bump into each other now and then, but that's about it. Maybe after we graduate . . ."

He broke off and walked rapidly ahead.

Why, Kate wondered, following him, am I jealous? How silly; I've got Pippa; why shouldn't Jon have a good friend, too, besides me?

"Look," said Jon a minute later, stopping, relaxed again. "Look at the partridge berries." He pointed to a pair of bright red berries, two of many dotting a carpet of closely nestled leaves that spread in tendrils along the ground at the side of the rough trail.

"Christmas," said Kate. "Red and green." She remembered seeing the same plant before, growing less thickly in the woods around River View.

"Right," Jon said. "People pick it and put it in bowls for centerpieces and stuff. But I like it better this way, the way it's supposed to be." He ran his hand lightly over the red and green mass.

In a very short time the trail, which led through woods vivid with changing leaves and open to the sky where some leaves had already fallen, made a sharp turn. Ahead, Kate saw what looked like a dried-up waterfall, rocky and steep, darkly roofed with overhanging branches for as far up as she could see.

"Here we are," Jon called over his shoulder. "Now it begins to get fun!"

"*There?*" Kate gulped, looking ahead and then dubiously down at her shoes; Jon wore heavy ankle-high boots, scuffed and very sturdy.

"It's not as steep as it looks, Kate, really. And we can take it slow. It's still early."

Early as it was, Kate and Jon had to step aside for two brisk young men dressed in shorts despite the chill, wearing thick socks and enormous boots and carrying huge framed packs and rolled-up sleeping bags strapped to their backs. They nodded curtly as they passed, without answering Jon's "Hi—nice morning." In a minute they were gone, scrambling up the rocky pile ahead as surely as goats.

"Wow," said Kate uneasily. "I hope we don't have to go that fast!"

"No way," said Jon. "We can even talk to each other once in a while, too. Those guys'll probably be at the top before we stop for lunch—unless you want to wait till the top to eat—and halfway to Maine by the time we're home. And I bet they won't have seen half of what we'll have seen. Come on, Katy—ready?"

For the next half hour or so, despite what Jon had said about talking, their conversation was mostly limited to things like "Watch it—loose rock" and "You okay?" when one of them stumbled. Kate found that her shoes did very well as long as she was careful to stay off loose pebbles; they clung to rocks tightly and allowed her to walk up them almost as if she were on flat ground. Her legs ached, though, and after a few minutes she was sure she'd have to ask Jon to stop for a rest before they got up even this first steep part. But in a while her muscles stretched out and she began moving more easily. She was in good general condition from running and found she didn't get out of breath as quickly as Jon. Despite his climbing experience, he was the one who finally called for a stop.

"Not much longer till the end of this bit," he said, as he paused with one hand on a gnarled tree trunk and one knee bent. "Then we can take a real break. Lunch, if you want."

"What time is it?" said Kate, pulling up her sleeve to look at her watch; it was, surprisingly, almost eleven. She'd thought earlier that it might be more fun to have lunch at the top than along the way, but as soon as Jon mentioned food, she realized she was already ravenous.

After a few more minutes of steep climbing, during which they both used their hands as much as their feet, Kate glimpsed sunlight ahead, and only seconds later they broke out into a steeply rising meadow, the grass interrupted here and there with flat gray rocks like giant flagstones. The sudden sunlight was deliciously warm and made Kate want to shout and run—but the meadow was too rough and steep for real running, and her legs, stretched muscles or no, badly needed a rest.

"There's a view," said Jon, looking to one side and slightly down.

Hills spread out below them, a town, a lake. A large bird floated lazily at eye level, above two white cotton balls of clouds. "We're in the sky," Kate said, delighted, and Jon nodded, his eyes shining.

"No one," he said, "has ever seen what I see quite as well as you. Thank you for coming." He spread his arms wide, embracing clouds, bird, sky, hills. "Isn't it stupendous?"

Kate spread her arms, too. Jon, pointing to the bird, shouted, "I'm an eagle, soar with me," and they both took off, sidestepping up the meadow, dipping and bending, being eagles in flight. And I do feel like one, thought Kate. I wish I were one truly, and Jon were, too, and we could stay here forever with the grass and the wind and the sky and the sun.

"Hungry?" asked Jon, soaring up to her, dipping his beak, folding his wings.

"Ummm," she said, remembering instantly that she was.

"There's a great spot over there." Jon led her toward the lower edge of the meadow—or the world, thought Kate. "It's off the trail, too," he said, "so we won't get trampled. More people will be up soon, I bet. Over here."

He pulled back some scrubby blueberry bushes and

revealed a small rock-lined indentation nestled in a hollow just before the meadow slipped abruptly down the mountainside; there were still a few ripe blueberries clinging to dry branches. "Okay?"

"Oh, yes," she said happily, slipping off her pack and letting the sun's warmth soak into her shoulders. "Yes."

"Shall we have lunch or just a snack?" Jon asked, dumping his pack, too, and sitting close beside her; there wasn't much room.

"I don't know. Is it very far to the top?"

"That means you're really hungry," he said. "Lunch, then. It's still early but we can stretch it out. And at the top—well, I'm not sure lunch'll seem quite right there anyway. We could save dessert for then, if you want, but we might not want it once we're there. It's kind of —you'll see. Let's wait and see how hungry we are. What've we got, anyway?"

They unpacked and pooled their food: oranges; nuts and raisins mixed together in a plastic bag—"We can save this," said Jon, putting the bag aside. "That'll be good for the way down." There were chicken pieces, too, lightly broiled, plus cheese and a couple of slices of bread with butter. There were also brownies, and Jon triumphantly produced two cans of warmish beer that sprayed foam when he opened them, making Kate laugh.

They ate looking down on a tiny, tranquil world: meadows, roads, and yards set about with silent miniature houses and even more miniature people, dogs, cows —hard to tell which was which at such a distance. Smoke drifted into disappearance from invisible chimneys, and doll-sized cars and trucks moved noiselessly along chalk-lined roads.

"A war," said Jon, "or even a mistake, would turn all that green black, and burn away all those orange and red and yellow and green leaves, and the houses and the cars, and nothing would move down there anymore because everyone and everything would be dead."

Kate nodded, shuddering inwardly.

Jon sang to her softly:

> *"Sail on, silvergirl,*
> *Sail on by.*
> *Your time has come to shine.*
> *All your dreams are on their way.*
> *See how they shine.*
> *If you need a friend*
> *I'm sailing right behind . . ."*

"So that's what it's from," she said. "Silvergirl. 'Bridge Over Troubled Water.' "

"Simon and Garfunkel," he said, and sang again:

> *"Like a bridge over troubled water*
> *I will ease your mind.*
> *Like a bridge over troubled water*
> *I will ease your mind."*

Then he turned and began stuffing chicken bones and bits of napkin into his pack. "Come on," he said. "The best is still ahead; we should get going. Packs'll be lighter now. Coming?"

Kate answered, "Yes," but she still lingered, looking down on the quiet scene below. This, she said to herself, is why my mother is a pacifist. Or was one. The greenness, the right of those cows to be there grazing, of the farmer to herd his sheep, of Jon to sing his songs.

Maybe I should come up here with Mom; maybe that would help . . .

"Katy!" Jon called impatiently.

"Coming!" she answered, impatient herself at the interruption.

But when she got to him, he put a gentle arm around her and they walked across the meadow like that, close and silent, and she knew he hadn't interrupted at all.

"Now," said Jon, when they got to where the flat rocks took over completely from the grass and the ground rose sharply upward, "here's where it really begins." He removed his arm from her waist and tightened his pack. "Shoelaces tied? Pack on straight? Knife okay on your belt?"

"Yes, yes, and yes," she said, checking each item, amused, as he mentioned it. She looked dubiously at the rocks ahead; they formed a giant granite staircase rising between thick granite walls. "Is this really the tough part? It can't be any worse than that dried-up waterfall. At least it looks firm."

"It's a different kind of worse," he said. "It's my favorite part, so it's not right to call it worse. But it's steep here and there; you do have to be careful and make sure that your shoes grip. And that your thigh muscles are working, and your knees. We used to call Hank's dog Spiderdog going up this part," he said. "She stuck to those rocks like some kind of super-canine insect. Hank and I were usually ahead, and the dog would keep racing back and forth between us and Hank's parents . . ."

Hank again, thought Kate. But she shrugged it off. Maybe there's something about everyone that no one else can know or understand. Maybe for me it's Hank, with Jon. After all, I can't expect Jon to understand me and Nick.

Not, she thought, irritated, that there's anything to understand anyway.

"Coming?"

"Yes," Kate said, and set off after him; he was eagerly striding across the first upward-sloping rock. It was perfectly smooth, like tipped-up asphalt.

The rocks went on that way, huge and evenly flat, sometimes spotted with moss and now and then with tufts of grass. Occasional rainwater puddles made little cups and bowls of ponds, each reflecting the sky's blue in its unrippled surface. Once, the trail dipped abruptly down into woods, plunging them into shade and sudden moist peaty fragrance, but it soon rose steeply up again, back into the sun and the barren stark beauty of gray granite, speckled here and there with white quartz and sparkling mica.

The sun was close and warm, but the air seemed thinner to Kate as they climbed and the wind blew steadily, keeping her from feeling hot. Kate saw other hikers, some nearby and others silhouetted in groups against the sky like desert caravans, but they all seemed as hushed as she and Jon by the endless world of sky and stone around them. When two people passed quite near, Kate's reluctant "Hello" was almost a whisper, and the couple answered with smiles instead of words—friendlier than the two men had been, despite the silence of their greeting.

In a while, after crossing a long ridge and becoming, Kate thought, a desert caravan themselves for anyone below, they came to a rough stand of low brush, blocking their view of what was ahead. Jon stepped in front of it, waiting for her. "I want us to see this together," he said, taking her hand.

Beyond the brush, the rocks stretched straight ahead and around a curve, making a high, flat road, climbing into the sky. Kate caught her breath in wonder as Jon pointed ahead to where the rocks swept sharply up, making a small peak. "The summit," he said softly. "That's another thing that never changes."

They walked hand in hand past scrubby evergreens hunched low against the rocks as if for protection from the wind, which was blowing strongly now, and past ankle-high miniature landscapes of feathery grass, tiny pools, and tree seedlings twisted into bonsai. There was nothing but sky above them and they were almost touching it, on a plateau between heaven and earth. People coming back from the summit seemed pulled into themselves and private, nodding absently as they passed; faster hikers going by them greeted them quickly and hurried on.

"Soon, now," said Jon, as they rounded the curve. The last bit, Kate realized, wasn't as steep as it had looked, not when one was coming to it, and even less when one was actually climbing it. And then they were there, standing on the very top of the mountain, the wind whistling around them, flapping the flannel shirts they had tied around their waists, making them huddle together in the sudden biting cold. In the shelter of tumbled boulders just below them, clusters of other people sat drinking from thermoses and canteens, consulting maps, looking into the distance across lower hills that stretched into the horizon. One man, Kate noticed, snoozed contentedly against his pack. The summit itself was small and surprisingly flat, sloping quickly down to several trails marked with ugly painted dots and crosses; Kate looked away from them and into the clear open sky.

No one spoke except the wind. No one looked at anyone else for more than a moment or two; there was too much sky. Kate felt drawn into quiet worship and peace, and her throat tightened, aching first with longing, then with anguish. We could be the last people on earth, she thought, looking around at the other silent hikers, the only ones left.

"A penny," Jon whispered into her ear.

She told him.

For answer he put his arm around her and kissed the side of her forehead—a long kiss, as if he were trying to send it into her mind to calm her thoughts.

"All your dreams are on their way," he sang, still holding her.

> *"See how they shine.*
> *If you need a friend,*
> *I'm sailing right behind."*

"Are you?" she asked, turning to him, her eyes wet with tears. "Are you, Jon?"

"You know I am, Katy," he answered. "I always have been. I always will be, no matter what."

"Will you help me, then? I want to go on trying, even if it's futile. Will you?"

He turned her to face him. "Yes," he said, holding her gently and speaking into her hair. "Yes, my silvergirl, yes."

⚮16

THE FIRST THING they decided to do was go to the River View police, both the chief and the youth officer.

"I wish I could help you," said Chief Laury, a tall, soldier-straight man with a thin mustache, "but you know the old saying 'Where there's smoke, there's fire'?" There *are* a lot of break-ins here done by Hastings kids, and . . ."

"And there are a lot of break-ins across the river done by our kids," put in Youth Officer Hendricks, who didn't look much older than Dan. "Or other kinds of damage, anyway. Sometimes I've thought we could be more tactful making arrests, Chief. We do assume a lot when we see a Hastings kid over here."

"I guess," said the chief, as the dispatcher came in with a message, cutting off the discussion. "But remember, resentment around here runs deep, and now with this waste-plant business . . ." He broke off. "Look, kids," he said, "I'm not sure your plan to end the rivalry will work in the present, shall we say, climate, but I'll do this much. I'll ask my officers to be a little more sensitive about making arrests." He showed them to the door. "Sorry I can't do more," he said. "But I wish you luck."

The next afternoon, Kate and Jon met with Pippa, who'd agreed to talk with the Hastings police, and who had come up with just about the same results as they had. "So the only thing," she said when she joined them on the View side of the river to plan, "is to go ahead and do whatever social things we can think of."

"And include everyone this time," Kate said, shivering. It was a gray, cloudy day and had turned damp-cold, as if it were going to snow, even though it was only early October. "Skid, Rab, everyone. Maybe Skid'll be on good behavior again anyway, like he was at the party."

"Why not have an indoor picnic?" suggested Pippa. "There must be an old barn someplace we could use. It's too late to count on being able to have a picnic outdoors, but we could borrow some hibachis and grills and stuff and make hamburgers as if we were outside, and toast marshmallows maybe, and have dancing afterward, or even something really dumb and old-fashioned like a hay ride."

"Not a bad idea," said Jon. "Kate?"

"I like it," she said. "Even the hay ride part. Isn't there an old barn out on Route 40, near—well, near Site One?"

"Right," said Pippa eagerly. "Perfect."

But Jon looked dubious. "That's Gretna's barn," he said. "Old Mr. Gretna. I'm not sure he'd let us use it. He's kind of cranky and he has a reputation for not liking kids. He ran me and Hank off his place a couple of years ago with a shotgun, at least we were pretty sure it was a shotgun. Besides," he added, quickly—Kate had just opened her mouth to ask him more—"since the first party was in River View, shouldn't the next one be in Hastings?"

"You're right," said Pippa, and Kate had to agree.

They both turned to Pippa.

164

"We're not big on old barns," she said slowly, "but maybe one of the churches—a couple of them rent out space for town functions. They might give us someplace for free, since it's sort of an ecumenical party. I'm not sure St. Stephen's—that's where I go—has room, but, oh, heck, let me ask around."

"Or maybe we could use someone's garage," suggested Kate, but that idea was instantly booed down when Jon said, "Who wants to eat hamburgers sitting around an oil puddle?" They settled on the church idea.

"Phase One," said Jon solemnly, holding out his hand; Pippa and Kate both spontaneously grasped it, then laughed, for the gesture seemed as silly as it did appropriate. "Phase One has been launched."

"Phase Two," said Kate almost to herself, thinking of the waste plant, "has got to come from the adults."

Friday night, trying to make it sound casual, Kate asked her parents, "How's it going with the waste-plant business?"

"Guest editorial," said her father proudly, holding up the local paper and displaying a headline that said, WASTE PLANT: IN THE FOREFRONT OR DOWN THE GARDEN PATH?

"Isn't that kind of a long title?" asked Dan, stopping on his way through the living room with a stack of books.

"Ummm," said Dad noncommittally. "Maybe a little. But it's provocative, don't you think?"

"Yes," said Dan, "and so's the editorial. I read it while you were taking out the garbage," he added when Dad looked surprised. "It's terrific. Congratulations."

"Thank you," said their father modestly; Mom looked pleased.

"Isn't town meeting in just a couple of weeks?" asked Kate, and then she quickly reached for the paper, saying, "I dibbs it next, okay?"

"You bet," said Dad. "And you're right about town meeting—in both towns, actually."

"Both towns at the same time?" asked Kate.

"Yes," said Mom, "according to the Browns."

"But according to them, too," said Dad, sighing, "Hastings people aren't very interested in working with us."

"Dad," said Kate, leaning forward, the idea hitting her, "remember what you said awhile back about joining forces? If the meetings are being held at the same time, why not hold them together? Maybe that'd get people more interested."

"Katy," warned Mom in her don't-ask-your-father-to-overdo voice.

"You're right," said Dad, slamming his fist decisively down on his chair arm. "It's worth a shot, anyway. It might just work! I doubt that it'd be allowed for a regular town meeting, but since this is a special one, and involves both towns—well, we'll see. I've been thinking all along that the state and the disposal company chose those two sites deliberately, knowing that the two towns are rivals to begin with—sort of to create a distraction from the real issues. Maybe if I push that point harder, Hastings'll be more interested in making this a two-town fight. River View, too."

"Go for it, Dad," said Dan; Mom smiled, but a little thinly.

"So maybe the two meetings *could* be combined?" Kate asked eagerly.

"We can certainly try," said Dad. "Where's my sword?" He patted his breast pocket and pulled out the pen and small notebook he'd taken to carrying around since he started doing research on waste disposal. "And when did you say, Ms. Kincaid," he asked, his pen poised above the notebook, "that you were announcing your candidacy for President?"

A few days later, when Kate was deep in preparations for the indoor picnic, which was to be held the following weekend in the Hastings Bay Congregational Church parish house, Dad came into her room and said, "Well, Madame President, we've got to go ahead with separate town meetings as scheduled—some regulation or other. But at ours I'm going to propose that a committee from both towns be appointed to work out a way of fighting the plant jointly. And your mother and I have talked to the Browns again and a few other people from Hastings and I think we've managed to persuade them to propose the same thing at their meeting."

Kate threw her arms around his neck. "Oh, Daddy," she said exuberantly, "you're great! Thank you! Now we'll really have something to celebrate at that picnic."

✂ 17

A BARN would have had more atmosphere, but the parish house—which Pippa did manage to get for free—wasn't bad. There was a spacious room on the second floor, a little like a gym, which Kate, Pippa, and Jon managed to brighten up with crepe paper, fall leaves, and some old lanterns Jon's mother let them borrow. Downstairs was a large kitchen with an eight-burner stove, plus an enormous dining room with long tables and stacks of uncomfortable folding chairs. "Like sitting on rocks," said Vinnie when he arrived at 7:00. "I'd rather use the floor" —but he helped open chairs anyway. By 7:30, when just about everyone except Rab had arrived, he was proved right; almost no one seemed to want to use the chairs, although several people perched on the tables while waiting for their food.

It wasn't long before Nick and Vinnie, helped by a tentatively friendly Skid, had cooked just about the last of the enormous mound of hamburger Kate and Pippa had bought that afternoon. Hot dogs were almost as popular, and disappeared quickly, along with rolls, pickles, and potato chips, plus several huge containers of coleslaw and potato salad. Kate finally began to relax with her second hamburger; by then there were so many loud conversations going on simultaneously that she couldn't focus on any of them. But that's a lot better than silence, she thought with relief as the people who were still downstairs moved upstairs and began to dance.

At about ten-thirty, when just about everyone was dancing and there were at least as many mixed couples as one-town ones, Kate heard someone stomping up the stairs and a moment later Rab appeared in the doorway, his motorcycle jacket dripping chains. He posed in the door as if making an entrance in a play, till everyone had seen him and stopped dancing.

"Hey, man, you got the wrong party," Skid shouted, momentarily breaking the tension. "The kids' Halloween costume party's back in River View. Next week."

Kate cringed but then realized that Skid sounded only mildly belligerent. To be sure, though, she called, "It's okay, Skid—no dress code here. Come on in, Rab."

Rab sauntered into the room. "Peace party, huh?" he said, looking around. "I guess I've just got to find me a Hastings Bay girl, then." He took a step toward Skid and Nick, who were standing together near Pippa and Vinnie, two Hastings Bay girls behind them. "Never thought I'd see you guys hanging around a *church*," he said scornfully.

Nick put a hand on Skid's arm; Skid, his face hardening, had taken a threatening step forward. "Never thought we'd see you around one either," Nick said quietly. "Hey, come on, man." He slapped Rab's shoulder lightly. "This is a *party*."

"Yeah," said Rab, glancing toward Pippa. He stretched out his hand, then grasped hers and pulled her forward. "So I guess no one'll mind if I make a little peace with Vinnie's girl, huh? We danced together pretty well at the last party, right, Pippa? Come on —let's try it again."

Kate held her breath as Nick's face darkened and Vinnie's hands clenched into fists. Pippa shook Rab off and stepped back, touching one of Vinnie's fists, forcing it to open. "Thanks, Rab," she said smoothly, her hand now in Vinnie's. "Maybe later, okay? Vinnie and I were just going to dance this one."

Rab stood still for a moment, a half smile on his lips. "Okay," he said at last, brushing her cheek with his gloved knuckles; Kate could see a muscle twitching in one corner of his jaw. "We'll make ourselves some peace another time, then, Pippa, right? Sometime soon, when you don't have your bodyguard along. H'mm?"

Kate saw Pippa's hand tighten in Vinnie's. "Sure," she said. "Sure, Rab."

Rab touched his forehead in a mock salute and strode to where Kate was standing with Jon, putting his hand on her shoulder before she could turn away. "Who forgot the music?" he asked loudly.

Someone turned it back on and Kate followed Rab onto the dance floor. She moved woodenly to the music, feeling Jon's eyes on her as well as Rab's, nervousness making her awkward. The others were dancing, too —Pippa and Vinnie at the opposite end of the room —but the couples were mostly View and View and Bay and Bay again, and the room seethed with tension.

"Not bad, Peacemaker, not bad," said Rab between numbers. "That's what they call you, right? Your Bay friends, I mean."

"That's right. One or two of them. My River View friends, too."

"Oh," said Rab. "You mean you still got some of those?"

"Rab . . ." Kate said, but the music started again and Rab, holding up one hand as if to quiet her, began to dance, forcing her to also. This time when the music ended he said, "Man, you sure are some dancer! How come I never noticed you back in junior high?"

Before she could think of a clever reply, Rab bent down, his mouth close to her ear. "Let's get out of here, Kate," he said. "Let's get to know each other again. Come on—you like bikes? Motorcycles, I mean. It's great riding at night, with just the stars and the road and the wind." He fingered her hair. "You seem like the adventurous type," he said insinuatingly. "And you'd look great with your hair blowing behind you." He held her hair out, as if illustrating the way it would look.

Kate managed a laugh, angry but also surprised by his eloquence; her mother's comment about his "hungry" look came back to her. "You wouldn't be able to see it, would you," she said, more gently than she'd intended, "if you were driving the motorcycle? Thanks, but I have to stay here."

Rab's eyes smoldered and he pulled back on her hair before he let it go; Kate's momentary sympathy for him vanished. Then the music started again and Nick strode up to Kate.

"I'm with the lady, Bay-boy," Rab said nastily.

"The lady's with who she wants to be with," Nick said. "Dance, Katy?"

Kate hesitated.

"See?" said Rab, taking Kate's hand. "Once a Viewie, always. . ."

"Oh, come on, Rab," Kate snapped, pulling away. "The reason we're all here is to get to know the kids from the other side."

"From what I hear," said Rab, his eyes narrowing again, "you've already gotten to know *this* person from the other side pretty well. Still, if you can't fight 'em . . . I guess I'll go back to making a little peace with Pippa, okay, Nicholas?"

"That's up to my sister," said Nick through his teeth.

Rab flashed his pasted-on smile at Kate, and said, "Just remember, Katy, you don't have to make up for your wimpy friend Jon by crossing the river. There's plenty of men on your own side." He slouched over to Pippa and began dancing around her; she was talking with Skid and Vinnie.

Nick frowned, watching. "I think I'd better go over," he said. "Vinnie's already steaming."

"I'm so mad myself I could kill him," Kate said, vowing never to soften toward Rab again.

But then she thought of her mother's reaction to Skid at the other party and wanted to unsay what she'd said.

Nick was grinning. "Some peacemaker. Told you it'd be tough."

Kate turned away. Then, watching as Vinnie said something to Rab, she retorted, "It would have been okay if he hadn't come."

"Now you know what I'm up against," Nick said. "Skid's bad enough—but he reacts more than acts, you know what I mean? You want to make peace, start with Rab."

"I—I know," said Kate. "I'm trying. At least I think I am."

"I'm trying, too," said Nick.

Kate smiled at him. "I know," she said again, then added awkwardly, "Nick, I understand how you feel about your folks, I really do. And the waste-plant thing. But if we could all just . . ."

A stifled scream from Pippa cut Kate off, followed by a few shouted words from Vinnie. Nick leaped away from Kate and grabbed Vinnie, pulling him out of range just as Rab's fist went out to punch him.

"Damn you!" Rab shouted, wrenching Vinnie away from Nick. "It's not your fight."

"She's my sister," Nick said. "And Vinnie's my friend."

"Stop!" Kate shouted frantically as people from Hastings Bay began clustering behind Vinnie and Nick, and people from River View, including Charlie and Ricky, gathered behind Rab. She saw Jon try to push Rab aside, but Rab shook him off as if he were a dog worrying a squirrel. Kate tried desperately to work her way between them, but Charlie reached out and pulled her back. "You'll get hurt, Katy," he said, his arm firmly around her shoulders. "Let the guys handle it."

"They're not handling it," Kate said vehemently. "I wish I'd taken those karate lessons!"

Just as hands from Hastings Bay—Skid's, Nick's—and River View—Ricky's, Jon's—reached out to pull Rab and Vinnie apart, the two of them surged closer and there was a quick exchange of blows. Suddenly Rab was on the floor, blood streaming from his nose, and Vinnie, his fists tight and one eye closing, was standing over him, as if daring him to get up.

"Okay, Vin," Nick said after a few seconds during

which no one moved or spoke. "You made your point."

Charlie let go of Kate and pulled Rab to his feet. "Enough, Rab," he said. "Time to go. This was an okay party till you came. Out."

"He threw the first punch," Rab said sullenly, jerking his thumb toward Vinnie.

"A technicality," said Charlie. "I'd have punched you myself in another minute. Out." He turned to some of the other boys, including both View and Bay as he spoke. "Gentlemen," he said. "Shall we assist Mr. Clemson from the room?"

Ricky and Skid moved toward Rab but Rab held up his hand; Kate was startled to see that he was shaking. "I was just leaving," he said, addressing all of them. "But look at you. First sign of trouble and look at you. Bay's on one side, View's on the other." He chuckled harshly. "It's not going to work," he said, turning to Kate. "Like I said, it's not going to work." He turned again. " 'Bye, Pippa. See you around. You, too—Peacemaker," he added sarcastically.

And then he was gone, storming down the stairs, and Pippa scraped together some dregs of raw hamburger for Vinnie's eye and sat holding it on for him. By the time the Hastings Bay youth officer arrived, saying carefully, "I got a call about a disturbance," nearly everyone was dancing again, View and Bay mixing—self-consciously and cautiously, but still mixing.

"Everything's fine, Officer Dolan," Nick called from where he was watching Kate and Jon dance. "As you can see."

"I saw a kid with a nasty-looking nose," Officer Dolan said, his jowly face suspicious. "Seems to me there's someone over there with meat on his eye—or am I seeing things?"

"You are definitely seeing things," Nick said. "Like I told you, everything's okay. A great party—doesn't it look like a great party? Everyone's having the time of their lives."

Officer Dolan looked dubiously around the room. "You call me," he said finally, "if there's anything you can't handle. Okay?"

"Okay," said Nick, and when Officer Dolan left, everyone clapped and Kate and Vinnie and Pippa and Jon kicked off their shoes and danced to the next song in the middle of the floor, with everyone else watching. They tried to get the others to mix partners similarly and join them, but this time no one did.

❧ 18

IT'LL BE OKAY, Kate told herself, jogging slowly to meet Pippa in the weak early-morning sunshine the next day; of course it'll be okay. Rab was just an aberration. The party itself was great.

—and a girl from Hastings Bay had said to her, leaving, that she'd tell her friends about it, and that she was glad to be getting to know River View kids; it was about time, she'd told Kate—

Kate, smiling at the memory, lengthened her stride and settled down to enjoy the morning. Running with Pippa was wonderful, both the companionship and the challenge they provided for each other now that Pippa's ability had just about caught up to Kate's. But Kate liked her first run along Route 40 from her house to the bridge, where she and Pippa always met, just as much, maybe even more. It's just me and the morning, she thought, feeling her legs stretch and her whole being expand.

She was hardly conscious anymore of her feet touching the pavement, except at the very beginning and end of a run, or of her lungs filling with air and contracting to expel it. Her mind floated above her body, especially when she was alone, noticing only what she wanted to notice, mostly suspended, unthinking—free.

"Hello!" she shouted to the day, nearing the bridge. "Good morning, morning!"

She was almost sorry when she reached the bridge and the end of her private run, but to her surprise, Pippa wasn't there—Pippa was never late and she herself, she saw from her watch, was certainly not early. A little annoyed, Kate untied her sweat jacket from around her waist and slipped it over her shoulders; she felt cold standing still.

A bird trilled above her, dipping down over the water, then flew away into the brush as a mournfully raucous honking drowned out its song. Kate tipped her head back to watch the V-line of geese noisily flying overhead, and wished suddenly for Jon.

"Winter, Miss Kettle," he'd said the last time they'd seen geese together, just before she'd left for Providence. "That means winter."

"Yes, Mr. Pot," she'd answered. "I know."

"Well, don't forget," he'd said, leaning close to her, but not quite touching. They'd rarely touched in those days, unlike now, when they often did or seemed poised on the edge of it. "Don't forget when you're living in that city."

She hadn't.

Still no Pippa.

Kate began pacing to keep warm, up and down the bridge, then across it and back. Maybe I should go to her house, she thought; something might be wrong.

Or maybe she just overslept after the party.

Yes, that's it; she and Vinnie must have gone someplace afterward. Maybe I should just go ahead on my own.

But even as she started off something told her to wait

longer, that Pippa would wait for her if it were the other way around, that she was being impatient.

Once more across the bridge and back, she told herself. Maybe a little along the road, toward Pippa's house. Maybe I'll meet her coming. She pictured Pippa running to meet her, her still-plump face (though she had lost more weight) shining, her curls bobbing damply as she ran. Seeing her gave Kate a good feeling, every time.

Maybe, thought Kate as she reached the end of the bridge, something's happened to Cassie.

Oh, God, of course that's it!

Alarmed, she tied her sweat jacket around her waist again and set off seriously to run to Pippa's house —but then thought better of it; better she go home and call. She'd get there sooner and a call wouldn't intrude so much if something was wrong.

Kate crossed the bridge again and automatically headed for the other side so she could run facing traffic —not that there was much at that hour. But as she turned, her eye caught something red at the side of the road.

Frowning, she went to it—it seemed to be some sort of fabric—and picked it up. It was a red bandana, speckled with white and black, just like the one Pippa often used to tie her hair back when she ran.

The bandana was damp.

Kate felt her heart lurch. She looked off the road to the left, where the bandana had been, now noticing that the faded brown ferns there were trampled, bent nearly flat, as if someone had passed.

Not ten steps into the brush, she found what was unmistakably Pippa's singlet, white, with a green number 4 on it. They had joked about it since it was almost identical to those the track team wore—Pippa's singlet, torn down the middle.

"Pippa?" Kate called tentatively, peering deeper into the brush. "Pip?"

And then she saw her, lying half hidden in the ferns, her bare back scratched and oozing blood. She was curled up, unmoving; her shorts were down around her knees, ripped like the singlet, her bra nearby, hooks and eyes torn out.

Kate's mouth went dry and she felt her knees begin to give way. I should get someone, part of her said, but the rest of her moved to Pippa, knelt beside her, touched her shoulder gently.

"Pippa? It's Kate. Pip . . ."

Sobbing, Pippa turned and clung to Kate, burying her head into her as if to hide there.

"Pippa, Pippa," Kate said, holding her, stroking her hair. "It's okay, Pippa, it'll be okay." But how can it be, she thought. How can it be, except that she's alive?

In a while, Pippa's sobs died away into long shuddering gulps, but her body still shook convulsively. She must be cold, Kate thought, untying her sweat jacket and covering Pippa with it as best she could.

They sat there in the brush as the sun rose higher and warmer, in silence, till at last Pippa moved her head slightly and, fumbling to pull the jacket closer around her, looked at Kate with eyes so full of pain and terror that Kate almost wept herself.

"Here," Kate said, trying to be businesslike, "let's get this on better." She took the jacket from Pippa, who moaned and closed her eyes as she did so; it was then that

Kate saw the bruises. "Put your arm here," she said, aching for her, dressing her as if she were a child, zipping the jacket, pulling up her torn shorts and fastening them as best she could, stuffing the limp bra into the jacket pocket without comment. "Okay, that's better. Now . . ."

Pippa grabbed Kate's arm. "He—he ran away," she said, her voice thick and choked. "He heard you shout on the road and ran away. "You—saved me. Oh. God, I was never so glad to hear a voice! Oh, Katy, Katy, I didn't dare call you, I . . ." Crying again, but less desperately, Pippa clung to Kate once more.

"Pippa, did he—did he do anything? I mean. . . ?"

Pippa shook her head. "He—he didn't rape me," she said, her voice catching on the word. "But he was going to, I know he was. He didn't say anything, just jumped out of the woods and—and dragged me in and hit me and ripped my clothes."

"Who, Pippa?" asked Kate, realizing that whoever it was must have been lying in wait for Pippa, must have known she was going to pass by—except Pippa hardly ever ran on the River View side of Route 40, was rarely so early that she had to run across to meet Kate— so it was *me* he was waiting for, Kate thought; oh, my God, it must have been me.

Or both of us. Or either.

"I—I don't know who he was," sobbed Pippa. "I don't know. He had something over his face, a stocking maybe; his nose and mouth were all mashed; it was awful. He looked like a monster." She seized Kate hysterically. "He could still be here," she whispered. "He could get both of us, he could have others hidden . . ."

"He can't be very brave," said Kate, swallowing her own mounting fear, "if he ran away when he heard me coming. I bet he's miles from here by now."

She hoped.

"Come on." She helped Pippa to stand, supporting her. "Let's get you out of here. Why don't we go to my house?" she said, trying to sound normal. "It's closer than yours from here. Or to the River View police station and call your mom."

"No," said Pippa. "The police—they'll take me to the hospital. I don't want anyone to touch me, not anyone." But she still clung to Kate.

"But if he didn't rape you, Pippa . . ."

"No, Katy, please. I want to go home. I want Mom."

"It's such a long walk, Pippa, I think I should get help —get someone with a car."

"No, don't leave me, Katy, don't leave me!" Pippa cried, tears spilling over again.

"Shh," said Kate, stroking her hair. "Okay, I won't. You're right, it'd be better for you to go home. We'll just take it nice and slow . . ."

A few cars passed them as they walked along Route 40, across the bridge and on toward Pippa's house. Each time one did, Pippa straightened up bravely and walked almost as if nothing were wrong. In between she slumped as if in pain, and let Kate support her with an arm around her waist.

And when about half a mile beyond the river they passed a pay phone Kate had completely forgotten was there, Kate was able to convince Pippa to let her use the dime her mother insisted she carry with her house key, and call Mrs. Brown.

Dialing, Kate hoped it would be Mr. Brown who answered, but it wasn't.

"Mrs. Brown," Kate said carefully, "this is Kate Kincaid. I wonder if you could come pick Pippa and me up? We're at the phone booth on Route 40."

"What's wrong?" Mrs. Brown asked immediately.

"Well—Pippa—she's okay, but she's had a kind of a scare . . ."

"Is she hurt?"

"A—a little bruised. But she can walk okay and everything."

Kate could almost hear Mrs. Brown grow pale and she prayed she wouldn't have to tell her what had happened before she was able to see for herself that Pippa was all right, at least physically. For a second Mrs. Brown sounded as if she was going to ask more questions, but then she stopped and said, "I'll be right there," and hung up without waiting for Kate to say goodbye.

In less than ten minutes Mrs. Brown arrived with Nick. Pippa started crying again as soon as she saw the car, and the moment her mother stepped out she flung herself into her arms.

"What happened, Kate?" Nick asked, getting out and walking around the car to her, stopping to put one hand on Pippa's shoulder.

"Someone tried to rape her," said Kate, cringing at her own bluntness. "But he heard me coming and ran away."

"Oh, my God," said Mrs. Brown, hugging Pippa closer. "Oh, my God! Pippa, Pippa, he didn't—did he?" She held Pippa at arm's length. "You can tell me. Please tell me—did he?"

"No, Mommy, no, he didn't," Pippa answered; her

voice was more like Cassie's than her own. "No—could—could we please go home now?"

"Yes, sweetheart, of course, come on." Mrs. Brown and Nick helped Pippa into the back seat and Mrs. Brown got in beside her, putting her arms around her again. Kate stood awkwardly at the side of the road.

"Who?" demanded Nick, facing Kate squarely. "Who did it?"

"She doesn't know," Kate said. "He had a stocking or something over his head, she said."

"Lucky for him," Nick said in cold fury. "I'd kill him if I knew who he was." He slammed into the car and snapped the key to its on position.

Mrs. Brown rolled down her window. "Thank you, Katy," she said as Nick raced the motor, his anger, Kate realized, going into the pressure of his foot. "Can—can we give you a ride home?"

"No, thanks," Kate said, touched that Mrs. Brown could even think of being so polite. "You get Pippa home. Just—could someone call me later and tell me how she is?"

"Of course," said Mrs. Brown. And then, as if still trying to be considerate of Kate, she waved as Nick noisily turned the car around and drove off.

Not allowing herself to think that whoever had attacked Pippa might still be waiting for her—but there would be people around, it was close to ten o'clock—Kate ran back over the bridge, and home.

✗19

SHAKING, Kate burst into the incongruously bright kitchen where her mother was incongruously peeling potatoes for Sunday dinner, and blurted out what had happened.

Her mother dropped her knife. "Oh, my God," she said, putting her arms around Kate, leading her to the table, sitting her down. "Thank God you found her, came along when you did. Oh, Katy . . ." Her mother knelt by the chair and held her hands, and Kate bent down and clung to her as Pippa had clung—except Kate's eyes were dry, though she longed for the relief of tears.

"I'm okay," she whispered in a while, patting her mother's shoulder. "I'm okay. It's Pippa I'm worried about."

"Why don't I call Mrs. Brown?" said Mom, standing up, but watching Kate anxiously. "You sure you're okay?"

Kate nodded, knowing that wasn't entirely true; she couldn't rid herself of the idea that what had happened to Pippa was very, very purposeful—and that she herself was to blame.

But maybe that wasn't true. Maybe there was no connection.

In a few minutes her mother came back. "Pippa's asleep," she said, sitting down at the table. She had a hot bath and then went to bed. Mr. Brown called the police; they'll be going over later to talk to Pippa. Kate? Are you positive she wasn't raped? Her mother wanted to know. I can call her back."

"She said she wasn't," Kate answered dully. "And— no. I don't think she was. She was still partly dressed. And she was hysterical, Mom; I think she'd have told me. I —oh, God," she said, beginning to break down at last, burying her face in her arms. "I can't imagine what— how she must have felt, how awful it must have been . . ."

"Darling, I think you can," her mother said gently. "Any woman can. I think that's one reason why it's hurting you so much. Along with the fact that it's Pippa —you've become so close."

Kate knew Mom was right. She *was* imagining it, every bit of it: Pippa's terror, her helplessness, her bewilderment that anyone could do this to her. Kate felt herself shake, then realized she was trembling uncontrollably.

Her mother got up quickly and went to the liquor cabinet, where she poured something brownish into a glass. "Drink this, Katy," she said as if dispensing medicine. "Come on, honey, drink it right down."

Whatever it was—whiskey? cognac?—burned, making her cough, but it warmed her, and the coughing distracted her; soon the shaking stopped.

"I think," said her mother, after they'd talked more and drunk two cups of coffee, and Kate had reluctantly eaten some toast, "that the early-morning runs will have to stop for a while."

"No!" Kate was surprised at the sharpness of her own voice. "No. If it was someone from around here, someone who did it because of our having the party, then they'll have won, sort of, if we stop running. If I do, anyway; I could understand if Pippa wanted to stop. But I can't stop, Mom; I can't let them win that way."

"You can, Kate," her mother said firmly. "I think you're very brave even to dream of going on. But I can't let you. Not early in the morning before there are cars on the road. The weather's cool now; you can run after school when there are more people around. Or you can run when Jon's with you; maybe he'll be willing to follow you on his bike or something. You'll still be running, after all; whoever it is won't have won on that score." She paused, then took Kate's hand. "If there *is* some link between this and the feud, as you and Jon and Pippa call it, don't you think it might be a good idea to ease up a little in trying to get the kids from both towns together?"

Kate felt her shoulders tense; not this, she was thinking; not this right now. Even if he was maybe waiting for me . . .

"Listen to me, Kate," said her mother. "I know you think I've compromised my principles by feeling the way I did when those boys came here to your party. But I feel the same way now. You are too important to me, to Daddy, and to Dan, too precious, for us to allow you to take that kind of risk. If it had been you . . ." Her mother looked away.

"Katy," she went on a moment later, "you've got to start thinking about whether your end justifies your means. Or maybe just about what you're willing to sacrifice to get the result you want."

"The result I want," said Kate slowly, fighting an exhaustion so deep that the desire to sleep herself into oblivion, like Pippa, was overpowering—"The result I want," she repeated, "is worth some sacrifices."

"Of *Pippa?*" said her mother, putting her hands on Kate's shoulders and shaking her gently. "Of your best friend? Your brother?"

"No," said Kate miserably, "but . . ."

"World War I," said her mother, moving to the counter and taking a second paring knife out of the drawer, "was supposed to be the 'war to end wars.' That has a nice ring to it, doesn't it? But it also doesn't make much sense. And it didn't work. You're a good pacifist, Kate, maybe a better one than I am. But don't let your principles make you foolish. And especially don't let them make you heartless. Don't risk other people's safety. Or your own." She held her hand out to Kate. "Come on, pal," she said. "I didn't mean to be so tough on you. Let's get at those potatoes. Then maybe we can —I don't know. What would you like to do? Aside from making dinner, which I'd love help with, I'm yours for the rest of the day, unless you'd rather be by yourself, or maybe with Jon. We could go to a movie . . ."

Kate got up and picked up a paring knife, but then leaned against the counter, ignoring the potatoes. "Do you really think I'm heartless?" she asked.

Her mother shook her head, rinsing a potato she'd just peeled; she dropped it into a bowl of water. "No," she said, "I don't, and I'm sorry I said that. Take it—oh, as a warning, I suppose." Her mother gave Kate a friendly poke in the side. "Hey," she said, "look at what happened to Joan of Arc!"

But Kate moved away. "I can't stop, Mom," she said, tears stinging her eyes. "I can't. Could you? If you'd gone as far as I have?"

Her mother turned, putting her hands on Kate's shoulders. "No, I don't think I could," she said. "But I think I might change my approach a little, although to be honest with you, I'm not sure what I'd change it to. Okay?"

"Okay," Kate said thickly.

Her mother handed her a potato. "You need a break from all this, honey," she said. "Time to sort things out. Really—what would you like to do today? I'm serious, how about a movie?"

"I think I'd just like to hang around here," Kate said, starting to peel. "Read or something. Rake leaves with Daddy—" She looked at her mother. "Oh, God," she said, "Daddy. Maybe—maybe we shouldn't tell him?"

"I was hoping you might say that," her mother said. "I want to tell him. And I know you do, too. But I'd like to talk to his doctor first, see what he thinks."

Kate agreed, and then they attacked the potatoes.

Late that afternoon when Kate was alone in the living room trying to read, Nick phoned.

"Thanks for calling," Kate said gratefully when she heard his voice. "How's Pippa?"

"Still sleeping. She's sleeping like she never wants to wake up." He sounded harsh, almost hostile. "The cops came and she could hardly talk to them. Mostly all she could do was cry. But she did say a little, Kate. She said you found her on the River View side of the bridge. Is that true?"

"Yes," said Kate, realizing that she was twisting the phone cord; she let it go. "Yes, it's true, but . . ."

"So see what your peacemaking did?" Nick said, pain audible beneath his anger. "See what it's done?"

"Wait, Nick," said Kate, panicking. "How—look, she said the man was—had a stocking on, that she didn't recognize him, that . . ."

"Yeah, I know," said Nick. "But she also said he was young, or she thought he was anyway, because he had a class ring on, and that it looked like the one this year's seniors have. And she said she saw something sort of gleaming in the woods. Like a bike. Or a motorcycle."

Kate closed her eyes.

"So the way I figure it, putting that together with last night, is that it's got to be Rab or one of his boys. And since not too many of his boys are seniors . . . Look, I just wanted to tell you, because believe it or not I still think you're a good kid and you're Pippa's friend and all and if—well, let's just say I like you, you know what I mean? But family comes first, Kate, like I guess you already know, at least in my house and on my side of the river. So I just wanted to say, too, that all peacemaking's off and so are the gloves. You follow?"

Kate felt sick to her stomach, but she nodded. Then, realizing that he couldn't see her, she quickly said, "Nick —yes, I follow. But you don't *know* it's Rab; you don't know it's anyone from here. It could be someone from Hastings."

"Oh, come on," he said scornfully. "No one from Hastings would dare mess with my sister, Vinnie's girl."

"It could be someone from another town. From Boston, even."

"With a Bay/View senior ring on?"

"But she was upset, Nick; she was hysterical when I found her. She couldn't be sure of that ring."

"She said it was a class ring. And that it had a red stone. You don't have to be calm to notice that."

"Other schools' class rings have red stones."

"Come on, Katy! It's a nice try, but I don't buy it. You prove it wasn't someone from View. Then we'll try peacemaking again. But till you prove it you can't expect me to let this go. I'm sorry. I can't let it go, you know that."

"Nick," said Kate desperately, "wait. You *can* let it go. You can. You'd be—bigger for it. I'd admire you so much."

"Would you?" he asked angrily. "Well, you're not everyone. And you know what? I just started to admire you less. You can call yourself my sister's friend and say I should let this go? A friend would help me find the guy, help me kill him, even. But not you, huh? You're like the people who try to make peace in wars. You know what they do? They forget that guys fight because someone messed up their country, or their city, or their family, or their friends, or their religion. No man can forget things like that, Kate, no man can ignore them. No man who *is* a man, anyway."

And with that, Nick hung up, leaving Kate staring at the phone, too numb for tears or words—except one word, her mother's: heartless.

She felt hands on her shoulders, and turned to see her father looking down at her. "Something's happened, Katy, hasn't it?" he asked. "Something bad. Your mother and you have been so damn cheerful all day I know you're trying to protect me from something. And now this phone conversation. I heard most of your side of it —forgive me, but you were so upset. What is it, Katy, what's happened? I'm not as fragile as you think, honey, truly, I'm not."

"I—I can't tell you everything," Kate said, forcing herself to focus on him. "I can't. Mom said . . ."

"It's going to worry me more not knowing, at this point, than knowing. I'm going to imagine things." He smiled. "Murder, mayhem, rape?"

She started at the word rape.

"I hit it, right?" He put his arms around her. "Not you," he said softly. "Please, God, not you."

"No, Daddy," she said quickly. "Not me—not quite. Pippa. And not quite rape either. Someone tried, that's all."

"That poor child," he said, still softly, still holding her —but she could feel his anger. "That poor, poor child. Oh, Katy, you must be in such pain for her, so frightened. That any man could do that . . ."

"I—oh, Daddy!" Her control slipped, and she clung to him.

But all through the rest of that terrible day, when her parents and, later, Dan, treated her as if she were made of rare china, the same harsh word kept echoing in her mind: heartless—*heartless* . . .

✳20

Jᴏɴ ᴡᴀs ᴡᴀɪᴛɪɴɢ outside Kate's door the next morning when she left for school.

"Your mom called me," he said, taking her hand, not even blaming her, she realized, for not calling him herself. She was grateful that he didn't seem hurt—though he does mind, she realized, watching his face.

He stayed close to her all day. I'm lucky, she thought, feeling undeserving; so lucky.

But she had little time to think about Jon. In the morning, the Hastings Bay girl who'd spoken to her after the party smiled at her and asked, "How're you doing?" But by noon that same girl, talking in the hall with two others, turned her back as Kate passed. Nick was controlled, but his fury showed in his eyes, which silently accused every River View boy who rode a motorcycle and wore a class ring.

Pippa was not in school.

Charlie Moss, Kate noticed, sat near her in every class they shared, not interfering, just there.

And Rab sprawled in his usual back-row seat in assembly, sniggering with his cronies—more than normally? Did he seem proud of himself? Hostile? Kate couldn't tell; he seemed to swagger more, especially at lunchtime when he passed her in the hall, and to look her up and down more brashly. Once he reached a hand toward her but Jon stepped hastily between them, and Rab, saying "Ummm-*ummm*," moved away.

Karen Anderson, the Pencil, faced Kate angrily on the field in gym class. "You and your ecumenism," she spat. "See where it's gotten us? My mother won't let me run in the mornings before school anymore."

"Neither will mine," said Kate, wanting to hurl the words at her as if they were weapons. "I suppose they're right."

"Right or not, it's your fault, isn't it, for being such a busybody? I don't see," she went on snippily, "how anyone who's been away for as long as you have can think she can come right in here and just take over. Some people have a lot of nerve."

Kate turned away.

Not long before the last bell, when Kate was getting a drink of water, Nick sidled up to her, leaning his arm against the wall the way he'd done the day she'd met him.

"Pippa's barely talking," he told her, "but she said to thank you."

"Give her my love," said Kate miserably. "Tell her she doesn't have to thank me."

"I almost did," said Nick, "believe me. But you did find her, even if . . ." He broke off, then said, "She's afraid to go out of the house, Kate."

"I don't blame her. I would be, too."

"She wouldn't even go in the car with Mom to see Cassie."

"How is Cassie?" Kate heard the woodenness in her own voice but was powerless to make it go away.

Nick shrugged. "So-so. The treatment's helping her hold her own, I guess. At least for now."

"I'm glad."

"Oh, God, you're a weird one! I can't figure you, you know what I mean? I can't figure me, either. I should be ignoring you."

"I'm glad you're not," she said quickly. "Can I see Pippa?"

"I don't know. I'll ask Mom."

"Could you ask Pippa, too?"

"I said," he told her angrily, "that I'd ask Mom. She's in charge of Pippa. Pippa's—the doctor says—Kate, when I said she's barely talking, that's what I meant. It's like she's half crazy or something."

For a moment he seemed to be appealing to her, asking her to explain, and she put her hand on his arm in sympathy. But she couldn't find any words.

"Vinnie hasn't even called her," Nick went on. "I had to spend half of last night keeping him and Skid from coming over here and practically burning River View down. Myself, too."

"Tell Vinnie to call her," Kate interrupted, appalled enough to speak now, hurting all over again for Pippa. "Please. She must need him more than anyone. Not to burn River View down—she must need him to hold her, to make her feel clean again."

"She is clean," said Nick stubbornly. "She didn't do anything."

"You're not a woman," said Kate bluntly. "You don't know how she feels. Tell Vinnie to call her."

"Listen," said Nick, so doggedly that Kate didn't know if he'd absorbed what she'd said or not, "I can't keep Vinnie and Skid away forever. It's Vinnie's way, you know? He's a nice guy, but—heck, he wants to marry Pippa. That fight at the party really set him off. Skid's still boiling about that himself. You know how he hates Rab anyway, and he's got a hell of a temper. They're both mad at everyone right now, everyone in View, you included, for that party." He went right on even though Kate tried to break in. "I'm just telling you what they feel. They think you brought the two towns closer when they didn't want to be close, and that that's what riled people up more, Rab especially. His fuse isn't any longer than Skid's or Vinnie's, only it's a lot colder. When he does something, he plans it out carefully beforehand."

Kate thought of Jon's back, and knew Nick was right.

"So listen. I'm going to hold Vinnie and Skid back as long as I can. But if I'm not around, I don't know what'll happen."

He paused, leaning closer. "Peacemaker," he said —was it sarcastically? "If you could find out if Rab did it, it'd help. Narrow things down. Then Vinnie and Skid would only have one guy to be mad at instead of a whole town."

Kate wanted again to sleep, to make the whole thing go away. Peacemaker, she thought; no. Not that. He's the peacemaker now. I'm just Bossy Kate.

And useless. Useless, heartless, Bossy Kate.

"I can't," she said, turning away. "I'm—sorry."

Nick seized her arm. "I respected you," he said through his teeth. "I really respected you, once I got over thinking you were butting in and being, I don't know, stuck-up, maybe. I thought you had guts and I thought you cared about people." He let go of her arm; it hurt where he'd held it. "But I guess I was wrong. No guts after all, not even the guts to finish what you started." His eyes were icy. "Okay, then," he said. "I guess I'll have to finish it. I guess I'll just have to find out for myself, or maybe let Vinnie and Skid come over here after all."

When you do something, Kate could hear her father say, *do it. Finish what you start. Don't leave off in the middle. Don't put off till tomorrow . . .*

"Wait," she said, struggling to rouse herself as Nick started to walk away. "Wait, I . . ."

"You what?" he snapped. "What? I haven't got all day."

"No," she said humbly. "No, I know you don't. It's just that I . . ."

No, Kate, she told herself. No good. Stop feeling sorry for yourself. You know he's right. *Finish what you start.*

"Okay," she said, pushing her hair back. The ends were damp, she realized, from the water fountain; it must be time to have it cut. "Okay. I'll try to find out."

Nick studied her expressionlessly, and then his face softened. He raised one finger to her cheek, touched it gently, and left.

But how could she do it?

It haunted her all that day. At dismissal, she avoided Rab, her heart pounding when he passed her in the hall, and the rest of the afternoon, no matter what else she did, his face got in her way.

Very late that afternoon, she decided to call Pippa, but Mrs. Brown said first that she was sleeping and then, when Kate asked when she could call, said she needed more time before she could talk to anyone—yes, even to Kate. "Even," said Mrs. Brown, her voice breaking, "to us . . ."

At dinner, which Kate barely tasted, Dad said that Elizabeth Briggs had called to ask him to delay his next article on the waste dump. "Says the climate's not right," he sputtered disgustedly, "because of what happened to Pippa."

"I suppose that's true, Jim," said Mom thoughtfully, dishing him out a second helping of beans. "It's an awful thing to say, but it couldn't help but increase the tension."

"So what're you going to do, Dad?" Dan asked.

"Finish my article, of course," he said promptly, "and send it to Elizabeth with a note about not giving up. If diplomats cut off negotiations every time there was a border incident, treaties would never get signed."

"Border incident!" said Mom; Kate felt her mother's eyes on her. "Jim, don't you think . . ."

"It's okay," said Kate, putting down her napkin. "Really, it is. Why don't I get the dessert?" And she fled to the kitchen.

That night, after tossing restlessly in bed for over an hour, Kate got up and went to her window, where she sat staring out at the nearly bare branches silhouetted against the streetlight glow from the common.

I still don't know Rab did it. All I know is that he could have, that it would be like him.

And I don't know that trying to get View and Bay

together made him do it, if he did. Something else could have, something inside him.

And—she rested her head against the cool pane—even if Mom's right that the end doesn't justify the means, the end itself is still good.

Silently, she watched the trees; the wind was blowing slightly. *The end itself is still good,* she repeated like a litany. *If diplomats cut off negotiations . . . Finish what you start . . .*

By the next morning, Kate had decided the safest thing to do would be to talk to Rab, not with the idea of telling Nick if Rab confessed, because then heaven only knew what Nick would do, or Vinnie, or Skid, but in the hope that if Rab had attacked Pippa, she would somehow be able to convince him to turn himself in. And at least if he swore he didn't do it, she could tell Nick that.

But she knew, as she slowly got ready for school, that the chances of Rab's admitting anything one way or the other were almost nil. Why should he, especially to her? And why should he turn himself in, for that matter? Remorse? Not very likely. If he turned himself in, it would only be because he'd be afraid she would. And if he were afraid she would, what might he do to her?

Kate didn't want to think about that.

You have no choice, she told herself, forcing herself to go on dressing. No choice at all.

Besides, she thought, trying to believe it, there's still a chance it wasn't Rab at all.

As it turned out, Kate saw Rab only twice that day, and both times he was busy with other people. It wasn't until Wednesday, after she'd made two more futile attempts to call Pippa, that she had a chance to speak to him, and when the opportunity came, it took her so much by surprise that she almost let it go by.

It was after school; Jon was playing soccer and Kate went to the bike racks to get her bike to ride home. But Rab's motorcycle and two others were blocking it. One cycle rested on her chain lock and the handlebars of the others were entwined with it in such a way that she couldn't get at her lock to try to free it.

"It's deliberate," she muttered furiously, storming back into the gym where she'd seen Rab and a few of his friends shooting baskets.

Rab, she was about to call angrily when he passed her, dribbling, as she walked onto the court, *your bike's on my chain.* Then she realized that would probably put him on the defensive, and she managed to say simply, after calling him, "I want to talk to you."

There were a few juvenile looks and whistles from Rab's friends, but Rab threw the ball to one of them and sauntered over. It was then she saw that this might be the opportunity she'd been waiting for, if she could only swallow her anger about her bicycle.

"Well?" he said, looking down at her. "What do you want?"

She tried to move her eyes from the red stone in his ring. "It's kind of personal, Rab. Could we go someplace?"

"I'm not leaving the gym. I'm busy."

"I think when you hear what I have to say you'd just as soon it was in private."

He shrugged and led her up into the stands, flopping

down into one of the scarred seats. "Well?" he said again.

"What time did you get up Sunday morning?" Kate asked, trying to ignore the fluttering in her stomach, her chest; it was what she and Jon had decided to ask in order to catch him off guard.

But if it did, he recovered quickly. "What the heck kind of dumb question is that?" he snarled. "It's none of your business when I got up Sunday morning or any other morning."

"Rab," said Kate quickly, summoning all her courage, "there are people who think it was you who tried to rape Pippa. I'm giving you a chance to prove you didn't."

For a long moment she could read nothing but hostility in his eyes. Then, poking an emphatic finger at her, he said, "I don't answer questions like that without a lawyer. You're just trying to pin it on me, you and your wimpy friend." He got up. "At least your peacemaking days are over, huh? That's one good thing." Suddenly his forehead was almost touching hers, his eyes so close she couldn't see them, only feel the heat coming from his body, his breath. "Listen, chickie. I didn't lay a hand on your precious Pippa. But I'll tell you what. She needed to be put in her place. And so do you. You remember that. You and that wimpy boyfriend of yours. I thought I taught him a lesson a long time ago, but I guess he needs another." Rab straightened up. "At least the real enemy's got balls. Sooner or later, they'll take care of all of you. Meanwhile, you better stay outa sight, especially you and the wimp. It's about time things got back to normal around here."

"Rab!" shouted one of the boys from the basketball

court, startling Kate into remembering, with relief, that there were other people present, even if they were Rab's friends.

"Yeah, coming." Rab put his hands on Kate's shoulders, digging his fingers painfully in. "Get the point? Or do you need a more graphic demonstration?" He dropped his eyes slowly down her body. "I don't know who had that shot at Pippa, but the same thing could happen again. Get it?" He shook her twice, hard. "You mind your own business, Peacemaker. You mind your business and I'll mind mine, and things'll go along like they did before." Releasing her, he turned and went back down to the court, catching the ball that was thrown to him, dribbling it, shooting, ignoring her.

But when she managed to compose herself enough to stand up, she heard a sharp command from him. The ball stopped moving instantly, and Rab and his friends watched her as she left. Just before she closed the door, Rab said something, and everyone laughed.

She saw Jon near the bike racks, trying to free both his bike and hers. "Damn Rab," he said as she came up. "Maybe if we *both* tug at this stupid motorcycle—Katy?" He studied her face, then touched her arm. "Katy? What is it?"

Trying not to tremble, she told him.

"I wish I could say he's all bluster," Jon said, twisting Rab's handlebars as if they were Rab's own arms, "but I guess we know he's not. And he must be mighty mad after ending up flat on the floor last Saturday. Not" —he kicked the motorcycle's front tire, and at last the handlebars popped free enough for Kate to pull them out the rest of the way—"what you'd call a good loser." Both of them pushed the motorcycles, toppling them, and then lifted the third one off Kate's chain.

"There," Jon said, pulling her bike out of the rack when she'd unlocked it. "Here you are, Miss Kettle, good as new."

"Thanks."

"Don't mention it." He rubbed some grease off his hands. "How about you go on home, fast before they leave. I'll come over later."

"Jon," she said, not liking the look in his eyes, "you aren't going to do anything dumb, are you?"

He grinned. "I'd like to slash their tires," he said, "but they might think Hastings Bay kids did it. No, nothing dumb. Get along with you, Miss Kettle. Hey, trust me!"

She hugged him impulsively, and he gave her an affectionate spank as she got onto her bike. But she stopped just out of sight at the edge of the driveway, waited a second, and then rode back, leaning her bike against the gym wall and slipping quietly inside.

Jon was in the middle of the stands, looking down on Rab and his friends, who were clustered near the basket, riveted on him. She wasn't sure if they saw her or not.

". . . dusting her clothes for fingerprints," she heard Jon saying, "and taking impressions of the motorcycle tracks. Hendricks says they're pretty close to a suspect. Hendricks also said that if whoever it was came forward and confessed it'd go easier for him, especially since whoever it was didn't actually rape her. So"—Jon turned and Kate could tell from his eyes that he'd seen her; he turned back—"I just thought you guys should know. Us River View folks have to stick together." He wheeled, going rapidly back up the crude steps between the seats and pushing her ahead of him out the door.

"You damn fool," he said. "You crazy damn fool."

"You're the crazy damn fool," she said. "Now they'll want to kill you."

"They do anyway. What difference does it make?"

"Was any of that true?"

"All guesses," he said. "I'm going to go and talk to Hendricks now. Want to come?"

"I wish you two would stay out of police matters," said Officer Hendricks, sighing, rubbing his chin.

"The thing is," said Jon, "that aside from everything else, this whole business is making things worse between Hastings and View—it's like kerosene on old rags. I think Rab did it; I also don't think he had any intention of actually raping Pippa. My theory is that Kate's coming along gave him a way out. He knew she'd come along sooner or later, and if she hadn't, he'd have thought of something else, or maybe even just left. I know him pretty well," he said, hunching his shoulders slightly.

Officer Hendricks frowned. "Any more to your theory?"

"Rab's nervous," said Jon, "because Kate's beginning to end the feud. And that means he's losing power. He can't stand that."

Officer Hendricks sighed again; Kate watched his face closely, for what Jon said made perfect sense to her. "We did take impressions of the cycle tracks," Hendricks said, "and, okay, you've convinced me we should try to match them with Rab's bike. But you can't dust clothes for fingerprints, Jon, and I hope for your sake Rab doesn't find that out."

"There must be something you can test clothes for," said Kate.

"Hair, blood, skin particles, things like that. But you have to match them to a suspect's to get anything useful. Rab hasn't done anything we can arrest him for; we can't just go up to him and take a couple of hairs."

"Suppose someone else did?" asked Jon.

"I'm afraid not, friend," Hendricks said. "We'd have no proof they were actually his. I'm sure you're honest, but your word just wouldn't be enough." He tipped his chair back as if concluding the interview. "We'll work on it, though," he said. "We'll work on it very hard."

✖ 21

SCHOOL became impossible, seething with misinforma-
tion. Some people, reacting to rumors, whispered that
Pippa was never coming back; that she was in a mental
hospital; that she would never speak again. Others said
she had been raped after all and so badly injured she
would never be able to have children—or that she was
pregnant.

Kate tried to convince everyone that Pippa simply
wasn't ready to be with people yet, telling them what
Mrs. Brown kept repeating to her on the phone. But she
couldn't deny that she was worried herself, though she
didn't say that to the others. "What do you expect her
mother to tell you?" Karen Anderson asked scornfully.
"She's not going to tell *you* the truth till she's decided
what to do about it."

By the end of the week, Pippa was still not in school
and Nick ignored Kate every time she tried to approach
him to tell him what Rab had said. Finally on Friday she
handed him a note; he read it, snorted, and walked away
without saying anything.

Kate spent the weekend moodily reading, going for
bike rides with Jon, helping her father and brother rake
leaves—and trying to decide whether there was anything else she should do.

She was no closer to an answer Monday night when she sat down between her parents and Dan in the elementary school gym for the special town meeting. Tables set up near the door displayed stacks of anti-waste-dump literature. Kate took a batch and listlessly looked through it, but it was all about River View, with no mention of working with Hastings.

As if he'd read her mind, her father reached over and pulled a sheet out from the back of her pile. It was a reprint of his editorial, and below it, a reprint of a letter he'd written to the editor the next week, pleading for cooperation between the two towns. But one letter's no good, she thought dully, even though she wouldn't have thought it before Pippa had been attacked. And neither is one person.

It didn't help any to see, as the gym filled, very few high school students. Jon was there with his parents, and so were Marcia and Charlie, but Kate saw only a handful of others. They've given up, she thought, as the town moderator, a rotund, Dickensian man with a placid face, stepped to the podium to open the meeting.

"We are here," he intoned ministerially, "as you well know, to vote on a nonbinding article asking us to approve the state's building a nuclear waste disposal plant in River View." He took a pair of glasses out of his breast pocket, polished them with a not-very-white handkerchief, and read the official article:

"To see if the voters of this town support and approve the proposed action of the state to take a certain parcel of land on the western river bank, hereinafter called Site One, bounded on the north by the Hastings River, on the south and southwest by River Road, on the east by town conservation land, and on the northwest by land owned by Lucius Gretna, said parcel to be leased to United American Waste Disposal Company for the purpose of conducting an experimental nuclear waste disposal plant, or take any other action relative thereto."

"Good grief," Dan whispered. "I'm glad I knew what this meeting was about before I came."

"That's why I never wanted to be a lawyer," Dad whispered back. "I never was any good at foreign languages."

It was funny, but Kate found she couldn't even smile.

One of the town selectmen got up and said, "I move that the voters of this town support and approve the proposed action of the state . . ." and he read through the rest of the article verbatim. Kate turned inquiringly to her father, who whispered, "A technicality. You can't vote on the actual article; you have to vote on a motion made under it."

When the selectman returned to his seat, the moderator looked up over his glasses; the room was absolutely silent, as if everybody was still trying to absorb the full impact of the words that had been read. "Before we begin discussion," the moderator said, "a few people have presentations. Mr. Steven Jaspers, of the United American Waste Disposal Company, has some slides he'd like to show us of his firm's other experimental plants. Mr. Jaspers?"

Mr. Jaspers, who was not the man who had spoken at the high school—wise move, thought Kate wryly—rose, and after a few minutes of fiddling with his equipment and the lights, showed ten sunny slides of harm-less-looking buildings nestled behind perfect shrubs on carefully landscaped grounds. "You see," he said, "we hire the best of landscapers, the best of architects; we pride ourselves on the attractiveness of our plants. As we think you'll agree, their appearance is an asset, not a liability, to any community. They blend in just as well as your average new factory or office complex. Even better."

"How nice," whispered Dad sarcastically. "Pity we don't have any of those for it to blend in with."

"Hastings Bay does," said Mom.

The next few slides showed interiors—rooms full of gleaming white pipes, dials that rivaled a spaceship's, and huge vats. Then came a slide of several smiling men in bright yellow coveralls and masks, working under a sign saying WARNING—CONTAMINATED AREA. UNAUTHOR-IZED PERSONNEL KEEP OUT.

"Now that's reassuring," Dan muttered.

"You see," said Mr. Jaspers, switching quickly to a slide of a vast cafeteria with clumps of people eating sandwiches and drinking coffee, "we take all the neces-sary precautions, along with many that aren't necessary. Our operation here, like all our other operations, will be at least ninety-nine-percent fail-safe. As many of you know, we've already tested our methods exhaustively in the lab; it should go without saying that we wouldn't move into any community until we were sure of what we were doing. And move we must—all of us—to meet the growing needs of the twenty-first century." He lowered his voice and leaned forward. "One can't set aside the remote—I repeat, *remote*—chance of a freak accident. We acknowledge that freely, and that's why our fail-safe percentage is a shade less than a hundred. But we have so many safety devices, so many alarms and ways of shutting down parts of the operation or all of it, that the whole thing really is as safe as houses, as our friends the English say."

As Mr. Jaspers straightened up again, chuckling at his own humor, Dad whispered, "Except of course for houses caught in a nuclear blast," and another United man got up and said, "Just one more point, Jack, if I may."

Mr. Jaspers sat down, wearing a self-satisfied smile.

The other man leaned against the podium, facing the audience. "We're aware," he said, "that the jobs issue isn't very important on this side of the river as far as actual plant construction is concerned. But, confidentially, you folks over here in River View should keep in mind that there'll be a lot of long-term engineering and high-level technology jobs once the plant gets going. I understand that a fairly large percentage of talent along these lines lives here in River View, and of course those of you in related fields are already aware of the prestige that goes with working at one of our plants. I assure you that all but the very top managerial and technical jobs will be open. And"—he winked—"I daresay none of you would object to the increased tax dollars a few highly paid scientists would bring to your town should our top people decide to move to River View."

"What an unmitigated snob!" said Mom.

"What did I tell you?" said Dad. "He's trying to drive

a wedge between the two towns. Another United man's probably saying the same kind of thing over in Hastings."

Kate felt too sick to comment.

By then, one of the selectmen had begun to address the meeting. "He seems for it," Mom whispered, looking horrified.

So did one or two other town officials. Most, though, Kate saw as the meeting droned on, were opposed. But it didn't matter; not one of them, it seemed, had any thought whatsoever about working with Hastings Bay against both sites. It was as if none of them had even read her father's letter, let alone considered what it had to say.

Finally the moderator called for discussion from the floor.

After a woman had spoken eloquently about nuclear accidents and a man had spoken less eloquently about devaluation of property, Kate looked anxiously at her father. He seemed relaxed, except around his mouth, as if any tension he felt had gone there. "Don't worry," he whispered, "I'm fine. Just waiting till most people have said their pieces. Then I'll say mine. Tactical decision."

At last he got up to speak.

"My daughter, Kate," he began, nodding toward her, "whom some of you know, pointed out to me after my editorial in the River View *Herald* that both towns ought to be meeting together tonight instead of on opposite sides of the river. That, it turned out, wasn't possible, but those of you who read my letter in the next issue of the *Herald*— it's also on one of those handouts you picked up at the door—already know what my wife and I want to say here: that this plant will be so dangerous—the materials it will contain will be so volatile—that it does not belong in or even near *any* residential area, or any body of water, regardless of how much the powers that be want to experiment with disposal in 'the crowded Northeast.' There are, after all, still a few sparsely populated areas in this part of the country, at least relatively speaking. I submit to you that neither River View nor Hastings Bay should have this horror in its midst. We all know, with due respect to science and technology and to the hardworking representatives of United American, that the proposed plant cannot be made absolutely safe; United American admits as much themselves. We also know that the experiments the plant will conduct are vital to all our futures, and that this plant and others like it must go somewhere. But our actions tonight, nonbinding article or no, can set a precedent for finding responsible locations for all such plants, not just this one— and *that* will put River View on the map in a more lasting way, a more important way, than having prestigious jobs or more tax money will. Mr. Moderator, I would like to propose an amendment to the main motion."

"What is your amendment, sir?" asked the moderator in a respectful tone that made Kate feel both proud and hopeful; her mother and Dan looked hopeful, too.

"I move that the voters of this town, opposing the proposed taking for a waste disposal site, but recognizing the importance of there being such sites, be recorded as supporting the appointment by the selectmen of a committee to join with a similar committee from Hastings Bay to study the plans of the proposed nuclear waste disposal plant and its site requirements and to propose to the state and to United American Waste Disposal

Company an alternative site not in a residential area in River View, Hastings Bay, or any other town."

The moderator's face was impossible to read. "Do I hear a second?" he asked.

"Second," shouted a voice from the back of the room —Jon's father? Kate wasn't sure. She also wasn't sure that everyone would understand the complicated words of her father's motion, but the moderator, as if sensing the same difficulty, said, "Did everyone follow that? If I understand it right, Mr. Kincaid's motion is severalfold. He is saying that you, the voters, disapprove of locating the plant in River View but realize that nuclear waste disposal plants are a necessity. He's asking for a joint study committee, consisting of people from both River View and Hastings and appointed by the selectmen —of both towns, I assume?"

"Yes," said Kate's father.

". . . appointed by the selectmen of both towns to look at the plans for the plant and its site, and to come up with a different location—not Site One or Site Two. And he's also saying that the site they come up with shouldn't be in any residential area, in any town. Is that a fair interpretation, Mr. Kincaid?"

Again, Kate's father nodded.

"A complicated motion," said the moderator, turning back to the room at large, "but I'll allow it. Any discussion?"

Hands shot up almost before the words were out of his mouth.

"Since the vote on the main motion isn't binding," someone said, "I don't see how amending it can possibly do any good."

"Oh, but it can . . ." Kate's father leaped to his feet, shaking off his wife's restraining hand.

"Mr. Kincaid," said the moderator smoothly, "would you care to answer that?"

"Yes, sir, I would," said Kate's father more calmly. "If we simply vote against approving the proposal, and if Hastings Bay does also, as I think we can assume they will, the state will undoubtedly go ahead anyway, but they'll have to make the choice of the site themselves —they'll have to choose between us, unless they have a third site up their sleeves, which seems unlikely. But if both towns vote to form a study committee, and *do* form one, we'll be able to present them with something concrete of our own. If we're quick enough, they might just be willing to listen, because we'll be offering them an alternative. Sure, it's a long shot," he said. "They could still ignore us. As I said, I think a lot will depend on how fast we work and on how persuasive we are. But good lord, something's better than nothing, and a negative vote alone really won't accomplish anything. This at least will be a start and will show a spirit of cooperation between the two towns. United we stand . . . No pun intended," he added, glancing at Mr. Jaspers, whose face was stony.

"Yeah, nice idea," someone said from the middle of the room, "but . . ."

"Sam Jarvis?" said the moderator—Ricky's father, Kate realized, turning around to look. "Please identify yourself to the meeting."

"Sorry," said Mr. Jarvis. "Sam Jarvis, Pine Street. Nice idea, Kincaid, but—well, maybe you've forgotten since you've been away so long and all, but there's a lot of bad feeling between the two towns. I don't think we could work together. I don't think Hastings is going to want to anyway, not after what happened to that girl."

"You're right," shouted a voice from the back. "Mr. Moderator?"

As everyone turned around, a man came up the center aisle waving a piece of paper. "Mr. Moderator," he said again, "urgent." He handed the moderator the paper.

The moderator unfolded it and read. Then he folded it up again, sighing, his expression even less readable than before. "Ladies and gentlemen," he said. "Since this is a matter concerning both towns, there has been, as most of you know, a representative from each town observing the other's town meeting. Our observer, Mike Reynolds here, tells me that Hastings Bay just defeated Mr. Kincaid's amendment, which was presented there also. And then they voted no on having the waste plant in Hastings Bay." He turned to the man who'd brought the message. "Anything else, Mike?" he asked.

"You might say their meeting was short," said Mr. Reynolds, "but far from sweet. There was a fair amount of talk about jobs, first of all—a lot of people did think the plant would help on that score. But even most of them thought the dangers outweighed that, especially when someone pointed out that the construction jobs, anyway, wouldn't last all that long and that there'd be far fewer jobs inside the plant itself once it opened. But what really did your amendment in, Kincaid"—he turned to Kate's father—"was that girl being attacked. Some people said they thought it was significant that George Brown, the girl's father, didn't present the amendment as apparently was planned. Several people said they didn't think they could trust anyone from River View after what had happened. One fellow even said he hoped the plant was over here, that it would serve us right."

"Those stupid hotheads," someone muttered, and voices rose throughout the room. Kate reached for her father's hand and held it tightly. Dan, she saw, was shaking his head, and her mother was very pale and straight, as if every muscle in her body had tightened.

"Order, please," said the moderator calmly above the growing noise. "Order! We still have an amendment on the floor. Mr. Kincaid, do you wish to withdraw it, given the negative vote in Hastings Bay?"

"No!" said Kate's father, shouting to make himself heard. "No, I do not! We can still show our willingness to cooperate, and we can still show where we stand on the issue."

Kate held his hand even tighter; she realized she had never felt so close to her father in such a grown-up way. "Good for you," she whispered.

He squeezed her hand back, but said nothing.

The moderator, after quieting the meeting down, called for a vote on the amendment, and Kate watched tensely while the tellers counted every row of raised hands, wrote the resulting numbers down, and handed them to the town clerk, who added them up. And a minute or two later, the moderator stepped to the podium, still without changing expression. "Amendment defeated," he announced flatly. "Do I hear further discussion on the main motion?"

In the buzz of voices that followed, Kate saw her father's shoulders slump, and felt her own eyes fill with tears. A moment later, though, he smiled at her and patted her knee. "It's not over yet," he whispered. "There may still be a way."

But the discussion yielded nothing. The final vote on the main motion was an overwhelming no, and the two towns remained as far apart as before.

Kate woke the next morning shivering—there had been a frost overnight—and pulled up her window shade on a damp, gray day.

She met Jon outside right after breakfast and, wrapped in scarves and jackets, they biked despondently to school along the river, which flowed sluggishly between the melting frost-bristles projecting from both banks.

"I almost wish," said Kate, balancing Jon's bike against her own while Jon knelt to tie his shoe, "that I'd never left Providence."

"I'm not surprised," said Jon, "but I'm still glad you did." He straightened up and took his bike back from her. "Kate . . ."

"What?"

"It's not your fault, you know. Don't blame yourself."

"It is my fault," she said miserably. "Or it might be, and that's bad enough."

"You can't be responsible for other people's stupidity. It's not your fault that Rab's an awful person. It's not your fault that Vinnie has a short fuse, that Skid does, that the adults can't work together. The feud's not your fault, and neither is what happened to Pippa."

"If I'd left the whole thing alone . . ."

"Then a lot of kids who've begun to see how destructive the feud is wouldn't have seen it."

"Well, I'm through with it now," said Kate. "No more interfering, no more meddling, no more Bossy Kate. I'm just going to be a regular person."

"No more peacemaker?" said Jon. "No more silvergirl?" He smiled wistfully at her. "You were magnificent, Katy. Who ever said making peace was easy? Or that everyone's going to end up loving you just because you're trying to make them love each other?" He stopped as if considering what he was going to say next. And then very quietly he asked, "Is that what you did it for, Katy? To make people love you? People from both sides?"

"Oh, no!" she said, shocked. "At least I . . ." She broke off, trying to be honest; he stood there silently, watching her. "I don't know. Maybe I did. Maybe that's what's been behind all this from the beginning—one big selfish ego trip, just like Rab's, one big . . ." She threw her bike down and ran away from Jon, skidding down the slippery bank, crouching by the brown water.

He ran down after her and put his arm across her shoulders. "Don't be a nut," he said, shaking her. "Don't be dumb. Of course it wasn't all a big ego trip. Of course it wasn't. I didn't mean that. If I had, I—I wouldn't have said it, at least not that way. I only said it to make you see it *wasn't* an ego trip, Katy, honest—that you did it for good reasons and that that's worth something even if you failed. The only mistake you made, I think, was counting on people to be better than they are. But you know what?" He tilted her face up and looked into her eyes. "It's when someone thinks people are better than they are that they become their finest. They rise to it. Like kids, little kids. You expect them to be bad, they'll be bad. But you tell them how good they are and they'll try to live up to it." He hugged her. "You almost did that, Katy. It almost worked."

"Where," she asked, smiling at him through tears, feeling his warmth through both their jackets, "did you learn about little kids?"

"Summers. Baby-sitting, playground sitting."

She took his hand. "Oh, Jon, I can't believe there are still things I don't know about you. I want to know everything, always."

"You moving away again?"

"No, but . . ."

"Then you've got plenty of time to find out everything, don't you? We've both got plenty of time."

But that, as it turned out, was not true.

22

WITHIN A FEW DAYS, each town had sent its resounding no vote to the governor, along with a carefully prepared statement outlining why the plant should be located elsewhere. WE WON'T SELL HASTINGS DOWN THE RIVER! screamed the headline on an angry editorial in the Hastings Bay paper. "We'll stop'em with clubs if we have to," the editorial ended, "and if that doesn't work, some of us still believe that Americans have the right to bear arms."

River View was no better. VIEW SITE LEAST SUITABLE, read the headline on an article purporting to be news, but as Kate's father pointed out in disgust, "There's not one point in it that couldn't be made equally about Hastings Bay." He sent an angry letter to the paper, and Elizabeth Briggs no longer invited Mom to "drop in."

Dan, who passed through Hastings Bay nearly every day on his way to Harvard, reported a new rash of bumper stickers. THE DUMP: OVER THE RIVER, THROUGH THE WOODS—AND OUT! said one. Another said: HASTINGS BAY: WE LOVE OUR CHILDREN—NO DUMPING, and there was a homemade one that made Kate's heart skip: RIVER VIEW GIRLS, STAY HOME! This last was sponsored by a newly formed "Protection Committee"; Nick wouldn't talk about it, but Kate was almost certain that he and Vinnie and Skid were part of it.

Again, River View was no better. DUMP THE DUMP, BAN WASTED NUKES—and, homemade: RUN ON YOUR OWN SIDE. During the week after the two town meetings, Pippa remained at home, guarded by her mother. Kate finally wrote her a note, saying she missed her and hoped she'd feel better soon. The next afternoon, Pippa called and, after thanking her haltingly and saying she missed Kate, too, repeated her mother's words: she needed more time.

All week, most Bay and View students ignored each other in school. Classmates refused to work together anymore on academic projects; athletic teams whose opposite-side members had at least tolerated each other on the field for the sake of the sport, or had even begun to get along, began breaking up.

"This is absurd," the principal said at a special midweek assembly, pleading with everyone to "begin acting like human beings again." But Friday afternoon, after a mammoth fight in the cafeteria, he decided to close the school for a week's "cooling-off period."

That night, strengthened by her talk with Jon—wanting, too, to reestablish some kind of friendly contact—Kate phoned Nick.

"I'm busy," Nick said sullenly when she asked to see him.

"Come on," she said, trying to keep her tone light. "Let's just say I'm accepting your invitation to go to the movies. Or to Green Lake."

"Oh, cripes, you are persistent! A date's not what you want. I know damn well it isn't."

Kate hesitated. "I think we should talk," she said, trying to be honest. "And I was also sort of hoping we could still be friends."

Nick groaned. "Persistence," he said again. But she

knew from his voice that he was weakening, and by eight o'clock that night, he was sitting stiffly beside her at the movies in Warton, away from both their towns. Pippa, he said when she pressed him, had been coming downstairs for meals, but still spent most of her time in her room or with Cassie, who was home from the hospital, and the kittens; she rarely spoke, and cried when anyone mentioned going back to school. Their parents, Nick said, were thinking of taking her to counseling.

It was, luckily, a funny movie, and within half an hour they were both helpless with laughter. When Nick slipped a tentative arm over her shoulder, Kate felt comfortable about it, and glad.

Afterward, she said yes to a drive, and yes to the beer he offered her when he turned onto the dirt road near the Hastings side of the river, stopping just beyond the circle of light from the last street lamp before the bridge.

They were very silent.

"What now?" he asked finally, turning to her in the semidarkness after finishing his beer and a cigarette. He crushed the can as if he were angry again, or at least fighting suspicion, and dropped it neatly into the little plastic trash basket he kept in the back seat. "Is this where we're supposed to make out? A little, just enough so you can get mad? A lot, so you can cry rape? Vinnie said that's what you probably want to be able to . . ."

Without thinking, she lifted her hand to slap him.

He caught it before it reached his face and held it for a moment before dropping it. "Okay, okay. I told him he was wrong, that you weren't like that." He scrutinized her, his face partly in shadow. "What do you want, then? What do you really want?"

"What do you mean?"

"Did you really call me up because of politics? Or Pippa? Or—you know—me? Are you tired of the boy next door, which is what I figure Jon is? Or are you still playing peacemaker?"

"I'm not tired of Jon," she said, licking her lips, which were suddenly very dry. "Jon's part of me; he always will be. But I'd be lying if I said I didn't—like you."

He put his arm lightly over her shoulders again. "But it's a little politics, too, eh?"

Say what you came to say, Kate, she told herself. Never mind that you *do* like him.

"Nick," she began, trying to choose her words carefully, "doesn't it strike you as ridiculous that you and I, from two different sides, can sit here in your car after laughing together at the movies, talking like—like friends? And at the same time the school we go to has been closed because the principal's afraid someone's going to get hurt if we don't all stop hating each other?"

"Not really," he said. "We're two individuals. But at school we're part of two packs."

"Shouldn't the individuals win out?"

"I told you," Nick said, withdrawing his arm and taking two more beers out of a paper bag behind his seat, "that this whole thing is out of our hands. Why fuss about it anymore when nothing anyone can do is going to make a damn bit of difference to the really important thing?" He handed her one of the beers.

She opened it but then held it without drinking. "You're so close to being such a great guy," she said softly. "But it's like you think being a man means being tough and full of blind loyalty. Someone pushes you, you push him back, because you think that's the only way to behave. That's how wars start, my mother used to say. And that . . ."

"Your mother," said Nick bluntly, "is a pacifist. You told me that before. She's a pacifist because she's a woman. Women don't understand fighting."

"Name me a war," said Kate, trying not to sound angry, "that ended without hatred. Name me a war that ended war, the way World War I was supposed to."

"Name me a war that didn't settle something when it was over," Nick retaliated. "Territory, religion . . ."

"Temporarily settled." She felt on surer ground now, and drank some of her beer. "You think the loser feels great about losing? Being forced to give up something outright instead of at least getting part of it in a compromise?"

"Treaties are compromises," Nick said. "Good ones, because everyone gets something. And some wars you have to fight. Look at the Nazis. Look at what they did to the Jews. There was no way we couldn't fight to stop that."

She put down her beer. It struck her that for all her innocent childhood rage against Hitler, she had never thought of him in relation to her own pacifism.

That's what Mom knew that I didn't, she thought, stunned. I never let myself. She thought of Pippa, and Dan, and felt ashamed.

"Gotcha, huh?" said Nick triumphantly.

"You—you're right," she stammered, groping. "But I still believe that most of the time—okay, not always —fighting's no good. Maybe once in a while, like with the Nazis, people have to fight, but maybe only as a last resort. I still believe that. A last resort." She paused, still trying to work it out. "Nick, look. Usually no one's one hundred percent right or wrong. I really believe that. Besides, if it's that absolute, that clear—if it were always true that one side's right and the other's wrong, how come so many people believe one side or the other? How come everyone doesn't always agree with the side that's right? Sure, I guess there are exceptions once in a while, but mostly it's not that clear."

"Boy," said Nick, "you going to be a lawyer or a judge or a politician or what?"

"Maybe all three," she said, though she'd never thought of it before. "If you moved across the river tomorrow," she went on, after a moment during which neither of them spoke, "the way things are now, you'd have to change your loyalty, not because View's any better or any righter than Bay but because that's the only way you could survive without being called a traitor. See?"

Nick took a long swallow of beer; Kate did also.

"You are the damndest girl I ever knew," he said. "Part of me wants to test if you're even like a real girl at all, or if you're some kind of strange—I don't know, what is it? Some kind of women's-lib type, I guess, some kind of feminist. The other part of me says don't touch, she's too good for you, too—smart. Right. Too smart." He rubbed his arm across his forehead and took another long pull at his beer. "This is going to sound crazy," he said, "but if I kissed you, would you be mad?"

She looked at him, startled. "I—I don't know. We're talking right now, about something that's important."

"But you wouldn't slug me?"

Kate laughed. "I might."

224

"So no kiss, huh?"

"You kissed me before," she said lamely.

"Oh, so you've had one, you've had 'em all, right? Now I could show you kisses . . ." He leaned over, tickling her.

She squirmed, laughing involuntarily, and pushed him away. "Be serious," she said. "Come on, Nick, please. I hate being tickled."

"Then how come you laugh and wiggle like you like it?"

Fury flooded her. She wrenched her door open and got out, walking rapidly across the bridge.

In a minute he was beside her. "I'm sorry," he said. "Kate—I'm sorry. That was rotten. That was sort of like the cop who tried to tell me Pippa might've wanted to be raped. I'm sorry."

"Yes, it was," she said, not looking at him. But she felt herself softening.

He stopped, blocking her way. "What do you want me to do?"

She shrugged, reluctant to say, to be Bossy Kate again. "Come on. You must want me to do something."

She drew a deep breath. "Okay. I guess I was hoping you could talk to Vinnie. And Skid. Maybe tell them we should all be able to discuss what happened to Pippa. Maybe we can come to some agreement, maybe even figure out what to do about it. All of us together, though, not just one side or the other." She managed a smile. "You mentioned treaties. Maybe it's time for one."

"Will *you* talk to them?" he asked. "To Vinnie and Skid? It's kind of your project."

"I—well, sure," she fumbled. "But don't you think it'd be better if a group of us talked? You and Vinnie and

Skid and me and Jon—maybe Rab, too. I don't know. It'd be risky, but—maybe it's worth the risk? If we could all just make up our minds to really try it, to try just this one more time . . ."

"Kate, it's—Skid and Vinnie might think it's kind of a dumb idea," Nick said. "But," he added quickly, "I guess sometimes dumb ideas work. Or aren't so dumb."

Kate realized she was holding her breath, and let it out slowly.

Nick grinned. "At least you're not saying we should all go on a hunger strike or something, like that peace guy in India. Gandhi. Starve ourselves into getting along. Fast till we're too weak to care."

Kate grinned back. "Maybe that's what we *should* do. But you—you'll help get everyone together?"

He sobered. "Persistence again," he said. "You are something else. Yeah, okay, I'll try. But Vinnie's very mad right now. And if Skid sees Rab, I don't know what he'll do."

"Skid's been seeing Rab every day in school."

"Yeah. And half the fights that *didn't* break out were between them. The only reason they didn't fight was because I stuck to Skid like a burr. Besides, school's closed now, remember? And Vinnie . . ."

"Vinnie's *graduated*, he's working. If he can't keep his temper, especially around high school kids, he's—he's . . ."

Nick chuckled. "I like it when you get human," he said. "Like when you almost slapped me back there in the car. Some pacifist."

"I *am* human," Kate said, close to believing it again herself.

He took her hand. "May I?" he asked gently.

She nodded.

"If I were Jon . . ."

"You're not," she said sharply, dropping his hand and walking away.

Again he caught up to her. "You fixing to walk home? Because if you are, I kind of think I should go with you. Or drive you."

"So much," said Kate, giving in, "for women's lib, huh?"

He kissed her quickly, and then he drove her home.

23

"Tonight," the note Kate found outside her front door the next morning said. *"Ten o'clock, to negotiate. At the river. Nick, Vinnie, Skid."*

Kate felt her stomach contract, as if an iron claw had seized it. But it was too late now to worry about whether or not she'd done the right thing.

She read the note twice more, then handed it to Jon, who had come over to follow her on his bike while she ran.

" 'Yond Cassius has a lean and hungry look,' " Jon said, quoting Shakespeare. He tapped the note with his finger. " 'Such men are dangerous.' Still, it's a start."

"I hope so," said Kate. Please, God, she prayed as she began running, don't let anything go wrong this time.

By nine-thirty that night, two bonfires faced each other across the river; Jon had agreed that the need for light and warmth was greater than the need to avoid the possibility of police intervention. Boats taken out of storage were drawn up on either side, for there was too much traffic on the bridge on a Saturday night, even in late October, to risk talking there, and it was important to both sides to meet on neutral ground.

"This seems so silly," Kate whispered to Jon while

they waited. "All that stuff on the phone about boats and seconds and spokespeople. You'd think we were fourth graders."

Jon put his hand on her shoulder. "It'll be okay, Katy."

And that was all they said for a while.

Kate watched the firelight, and the flames shining on the water, and tried to tell herself that despite the childish trappings, this plan had a better chance of working than anything else—certainly a better chance, now, than more parties . . .

There was a rustling behind them and Charlie Moss appeared. He nodded without speaking and squatted down, holding his hands out to the fire. "Still no sign of Rab?" Charlie whispered, and Kate, worried, shook her head.

"Damn," said Charlie, looking at his watch. "It took me two hours of alternating between scare tactics and ego-feeding to get him to agree to come. I think I even said 'alleged near-rapist' or something like that a couple of times. I'm sorry, Kate. I guess he might not show."

"Might be just as well," said Jon grimly. "Except for his being the person who most of this is about, I can't see that he's going to be much use."

They fell into an uneasy silence, watching the bonfire across the river and listening to the small sounds that came from there: voices, the grating of boats against sand, a muffled splash or two. And then Rab burst through the underbrush and strode flamboyantly to the fire, as if he'd come to take part in a spectacle in which he himself was the star. But Kate sensed fear under his bravado.

"Remember," Charlie whispered to Rab as the town

clock struck ten in the distance and they climbed down the riverbank to launch the boats, "we're here to talk, not fight."

"And," said Jon, "remember it's Kate who talks for our side, or starts to, anyway."

"Yeah, yeah," said Rab. "She *starts*. But I've got things to say, too. *I* finish. And just in case . . ." He put his hand under his jacket and pulled out a small hunting knife, its blade flashing in the firelight.

Charlie reached for it, but Rab twisted away and returned the knife to the sheath Kate now saw he was wearing on his belt. "For emergencies, man," Rab said. "For emergencies."

"You'd better let us decide what's an emergency," said Charlie. "Right, Jon?"

"Right," said Jon. He bent down, still watching Rab, and untied a boat.

"Why don't you let one of us keep the knife?" asked Kate, wishing she didn't feel so cold—but it was tension, she knew; no—fear.

"No one touches this knife," said Rab. "No one but me. Anyone who tries feels its bite. Let's go. They're coming." He reached for the other boat's bow line.

Kate glanced across the river. Two boats were sliding noiselessly toward them.

"Must've oiled their oarlocks," said Jon lightly, motioning Kate to get into the boat he'd untied. Charlie and Rab climbed into the other.

"Or wrapped them," said Charlie as he and Jon each took up their oars. "My brother and I used to do that, wrap our oars in rags to muffle them. It worked pretty well . . ."

His voice trailed off into the heavy silence, broken only by the quiet sound of careful rowing.

For a minute Kate had an absurd desire to laugh; again, the whole thing seemed ridiculous. Is this how ambassadors feel, she wondered, as if they're playing a game? Or do they take themselves as seriously as the people who fight do?

Then all four boats were in the center of the river, and no one seemed to know what to do. Vinnie and Nick were in one Hastings boat; Skid in the other. Kate could see the shapes of other people gathering around the Hastings Bay fire. She looked back at River View and saw shapes there, too. Pippa, she thought, turning around again, eyes straining across the water; I wonder if Pippa's there—but no, of course she wouldn't be.

"So let's talk," came Nick's voice, brusque, out of the darkness. "We can't hold these boats still all night."

"Right," said Vinnie. "Let's get it over with."

Everyone looked at Kate.

Her mouth felt like sandpaper. "You guys sent the note," she said. "Would you like to start?"

Skid looked embarrassed; they all did, as if the childish setting and situation had defused them, even Rab, at least for the moment.

"It was your idea, Peacemaker," Vinnie said. "Seems to me you go first."

"Well," said Kate carefully, "I—we—River View people, I mean—agree with you that what happened to Pippa was terrible, whoever did it. We want you to know that, first of all. And we also want you to know that we agree that the person who did it should be punished, no matter where he's from. But the thing is . . ."

"We'll accept a confession," interrupted Vinnie loudly, as if he'd rehearsed it. "Nothing less. A confession. Otherwise it'll go on as it's been. View and Bay for themselves."

"But what if no one . . ." began Kate, but Jon put a hand on her arm.

"If someone does confess," asked Jon, "what then?"

"Then you turn him over to us," said Skid.

"For you to beat up?" said Charlie, backing water a bit more vigorously than the others. "Come on, man. How about we notify the cops? Or get him to turn himself in to the cops?"

"What if the cops don't buy your story?" asked Vinnie. "And what if the guy doesn't turn himself in? We haven't seen him do it so far, have we?"

"Remember," said Kate, taking a deep breath, "it might not be anyone in either town."

"Oh, yeah?" Vinnie looked pointedly at Charlie and Rab's boat. "I don't think so. A confession," he said, positioning his oars one forward, one back, as if to turn around. "That's our terms."

Rab leaned toward him abruptly, making his boat rock. "You worm," he said through clenched teeth. "You worm! Will you stop looking at me like that? You heard what the lady said. Maybe it's not anyone from either town. Or maybe—maybe it's someone from *your* town, someone who did it to make things look bad for us. Hell, maybe it's you, Skid, maybe . . ."

Skid plunged his oars into the water and pulled for Rab's boat. Rab laughed; Charlie began to row away, toward the River View shore.

"Stop!" Nick commanded in a voice so authoritative

that both Charlie and Skid stopped rowing; Charlie turned his boat to face Nick and Vinnie's, still keeping his distance from Skid's boat. "We didn't even hear any of that. No one's accusing anyone; we're looking for a confession."

"Forcing one, you mean," Rab shouted. "Trouble is, I didn't do it. Hell, who'd want a Hastings Bay girl?"

"You seemed interested enough at the party, Rab," said Jon quietly.

"Stow it, wimp," said Rab.

"Look"—Kate leaned forward—"I still think it'd be better if . . ."

"Shut up, Peacemaker," said Vinnie sharply. "It's not your battle anymore."

"Vinnie," Nick said, a warning in his voice.

"Watch who you say shut up to," said Jon angrily.

"Shut up, shut up, shut up!" Rab screeched, out of control. "If it weren't for her . . ."

"Oh, for Christ's sake!" Skid moved his boat closer; all four boats were in a circle now, clustered in the center of the river, sliding on its surface like giant menacing waterbugs. "Let's just grab him, Vinnie. He'll confess all right then." He pulled sharply on his oars as he spoke, shooting his boat toward Rab's; Rab, Kate saw, reached for his knife.

"No!" Kate tried to grab the oars from Jon.

"*Will* you get out of the way?" shouted Skid, ramming her boat with his—ramming it just as Jon darted between Kate and the oar Skid was waving.

And then Jon slipped.

Kate saw it all in slow motion: Jon grabbing futilely at the air, then toppling from the boat into the dark water, catching Skid's oar on the side of his head, sliding under—

For a fraction of a second there was absolutely no sound.

Then Kate leaped to her feet, screaming, "He can't swim!" Her boat rocked crazily. "He can't swim!" Clumsy with fear, she pulled at her shoes, her heavy jacket—but Charlie and Nick were quicker, both of them diving in, accidentally interfering with each other in their frantic effort to find Jon.

"Light!" Charlie called, surfacing. "For God's sake, light!"

Kate groped for the flashlight she'd put into the bow of the boat, found it, turned it on, swept it over the water—but there was nothing except an ever-widening circle of ripples.

"There!" cried Nick and dove into the circle.

But he came up with nothing.

A moment later Jon's head appeared at the outer edge of the circle, bobbing up once—then, as Kate screamed "There!" it went down again.

Nick and Charlie swam for him; Vinnie followed them slowly in his boat, being careful, Kate thought woodenly, not to go directly over where Jon might be, where he might come up. Rab sat hunched over, not moving; the fourth boat, Skid's, unnoticed, headed quietly downriver.

Nick dove, and called to Charlie as he came up; in seconds they were both swimming to shore, dragging something between them.

Kate, with a cry that was more a choke than a sob, seized the oars and followed as fast as she could.

But when she got to him, Jon was lying on his back on the bridge in a pool of water, his chest still, his eyes closed, his face as coldly pale as the light from the street lamp that shone on it.

❧24

"ONE AND TWO and three and four and five and six . . ."
Kate counted, compressing Jon's lower chest mechanically with her joined fists as she'd compressed her father's, over and over again, stopping every fifteen strokes
to cover Jon's mouth with hers, breathing her breath
into his lungs (he had vomited a little water; she had
turned his head to one side; she had kept him from choking). Then she moved back to his chest, not seeing or
hearing the growing crowd on the bridge, not conscious
of their words ("I called an ambulance"; "I called the fire
department"; "What happened, anyway?" "Shouldn't
someone notify his family?"), conscious only of Jon and
herself, of kissing his cold mouth, of her tears spilling
onto his closed eyelids . . .

"Two-man," said a voice, giving the CPR signal for a
double effort at resuscitation, and Kate, not even looking
at the slight dark-haired boy who had run up to her and
knelt beside Jon, nodded and counted with him, somehow remembering how to institute two-man, letting the
boy take over the chest compressions while she worked
on the breathing.

Then they switched.

Then they switched again.

And after—how many switches? Kate lost track

—Jon still lay there, apparently unconscious, unable to breathe on his own, his heart beating only when Kate and the dark-haired boy forced it to. If only I could take his heart out, Kate thought irrationally, if I could talk to it, soothe it, warm it into beating. Oh, Jon, Jon, she cried to him silently; Jon, don't be dead, don't die for this, for these terrible people, for this foolish fight, for my stupidity. Jon—Jon, my love, don't die . . .

"Here, miss, we'll take him now."

She hadn't heard the ambulance drive up, hadn't seen the EMTs step down with a stretcher, hadn't heard them ask the crowd, "How long?"—hadn't heard the answer: "Fifteen, twenty minutes."

She wouldn't move away from him, though the dark-haired boy, hesitating, looked up. The only thing in her mind now was the part of her training that said, "Don't stop once you've started; whatever you do, don't stop." She'd forgotten the rest of it: "But you may stop when competent help comes . . ."

One of the EMTs put his hand on her shoulder and said, "I'm an EMT, miss; so's my buddy, here. We'll take care of him now; you must be tired, stop."

Still Kate didn't move, even when someone said, "Come on, Hank," to the dark-haired boy and he, his face wet with tears, moved away; Kate switched easily back into one-man.

The EMT commanded sharply, "Two-man," and Kate, obeying instinctively again, let him join her. A few seconds later, his partner said, "Two-man—I'll take your place, miss, you're worn out," and Kate looked up, startled, because she hadn't expected that, had expected only to go on breathing and pumping life into Jon forever, to

237

die beside him when her own breath gave out. When she looked up, the second EMT nodded, and Nick put his arms around her and lifted her up.

She saw what was around her as if in a dream: the crowd of ashen-faced teenagers from both sides of the river; the whirling ambulance lights; the dark boy at the side of the bridge, his back to everyone, sobbing; the EMTs lifting Jon into the ambulance; the ambulance driving away—slowly, as if there were no hurry. It's kind of them to drive so gently, she thought, in case he's in pain . . .

Then again she felt the coldness of Jon's face against hers and the sodden stillness of his body. She heard someone scream and scream and go on screaming until she felt a slap on her cheek. Nick's voice said brokenly into her ear, "I'm sorry, I'm sorry, Katy. Baby, I didn't want to hurt you, but you were hysterical. Katy, Katy, cry now. Go on, baby, cry." She felt herself being led away, put into a car, and, awareness slowly returning, she realized Nick was driving and that Charlie Moss was on the other side of her, and she almost laughed. All we need, she thought, is Vinnie and Skid in the back seat, and Rab, and Jon . . .

When Kate woke up, the sun was shining outside her window, around and under the partly drawn shade, and her mother was sitting next to her, holding her hand. How odd, she thought; Mom hasn't done that since I had my appendix out when I was eleven. For a moment she lay with eyes half closed, enjoying her mother's touch and the sun and the two or three chickadees chirping outside at the bird feeder—and then she remembered and closed her eyes tightly again, wanting to die.

Her mother's voice, gentle but insistent, cut through. "Kate," she was saying, "Kate, Katy, you did all you could. No one could have done more. No one, Kate, could have saved him; the EMTs said so; no one."

Kate opened her eyes, cold certainty flooding her whole being, and she knew why she hadn't wanted to wake, for she knew then that she'd still somehow hoped he was alive. She knew that all night even in her sleep she'd been willing him to live, half believing it would work, repeating, "Breathe, Jon; in, out; in, out. Mr. Pot —come on, breathe."

"Oh, Katy." Her mother took Kate in her arms, lifting her a little off the bed and rocking her as if she were a baby. "Kate, Katy," her mother repeated over and over again. "Oh, God, if I could only reach you! Sweetie, sweetie, please cry, please say something—talk about it —tell me how it happened."

But Kate, like Pippa earlier, found there was nothing to say.

All day she lay in her room. Her mother brought her food, which she couldn't eat; her mother raised and lowered the shades; she turned on the radio and turned it off again. Dan looked in, bringing her flowers; her father read poetry to her, but she could barely hear the words. Finally night came, and they all left her alone.

She slipped into sleep gratefully, for Jon was there with her then, laughing, sunlight on his blond hair, summer-dark freckles clustered across his sunburned nose. At first they were both sixth graders again, then they were younger, third grade, maybe; then second:

". . . the pot calling the kettle black!"

"Miss Kettle!"

"Mr. Pot!"

Miss Kettle . . . Miss Kettle . . . Silvergirl . . . I'm sailing right behind . . .

"Are you, Jon?" she whispered. "Will you be? I can't go on alone, Jon, I can't. I don't even know where I'm going anymore, or if I am . . ."

He smiled. His face was older now, as it had been on Monadnock, and again she felt him kiss her, more lightly, though, like a soft breeze. "I'm with you, Katy," he seemed to say. "With you—with you—always."

She woke, half expecting to see him beside her, and then she turned onto her stomach and cried bitterly, like a child. She knew that although it was true he was with her now and would be with her for the rest of her life, she would never touch him or see him or talk with him again.

25

THERE WAS AN inquest before the funeral; Kate was still dazed when she went to it and she remembered nothing about it when it was over. "Death by accidental drowning" was the verdict.

She was dazed at the funeral, too, but about halfway through the service, she became aware enough to look around and she was surprised to see so many people from both towns. Nick was there, and beside him, very pale and much thinner, was Pippa, and next to her, paler still but giving Kate the faintest of smiles, was Cassie. Vinnie was beside Cassie, and behind him, stiff and sober-looking, was Skid.

Kate fought down nausea, but forced herself to go on looking around. "Innocence," the minister was saying, "Innocent victim . . ." There was Charlie, there was Carol, and Marcia, and Ricky, and even Karen, with Becky—a lot of people in their class from both sides of the river, she realized—and the dark boy from the bridge; she remembered his name, Hank, and for the first time was aware that he must be Jon's old friend. She studied him, trying to read something in his face— but what?

Two pews behind him was—oh, God—Rab . . .

"Forgive us our trespasses," said the minister, "as we forgive those . . ."

Kate clenched her fists. Forgive, yes, that's what I'm supposed to do. Forgive. Make peace. Dad calls his pen his sword. The pen is mightier. Your swords into plowshares. Study war no more . . .

". . . lesson in humility," the minister was saying now. "In brotherhood . . ."

Without thinking about it, Kate felt herself stand. She watched herself as if from a foot or two behind as she slid out of her pew and walked down the aisle past the startled congregation to the front of the church, which was now oddly silent except for her mother's voice saying "Kate" from what seemed a great distance away. Kate walked to Jon's coffin, to where Jon was lying (she supposed) under white wood (because he's a virgin, her mind told her; a virgin like me. Oh, God, I wish we'd . . .). Then her voice broke through the silence, surprising her. It must be my voice, she thought, because no one else is talking.

"Brotherhood," she heard herself say. "Yes." She paused, waiting to see what she would say next. "My mother told me once," she said at last, her mind clearing, "about a town that had a dangerous street corner in it. Some of the people asked for a SLOW—CHILDREN AT PLAY sign. But they were told they couldn't have one unless there was a bad accident—maybe two, or maybe a fatality." She said the word "fatality" carefully, her mind echoing it, whispering, *Jon's a fatality, Jon* . . .

She pushed the whisper aside.

"Well," she heard herself go on, "about a year later, a

child was killed at that corner, and then the people got their sign." She looked down at the coffin, then touched it, smoothing the wood under her fingers. "I guess my friend Jon is like that child—aren't you, Jon?" She looked up again. "When Jon and I were little, we didn't know we were supposed to hate people from Hastings Bay. And when I came back after being away for four years, I still didn't know it. But Jon did. He knew, and he didn't want any part of it. But he helped me to understand it, and then he helped me try to make peace. The main reason Jon was at the river that night was because of me, because he wanted peace, too."

Her eyes felt wet; the pews and the people were blurred. But not Jon's coffin. That was very clear.

"I guess the mother of the child who got killed at that dangerous corner," she said, trying desperately to keep her voice from breaking, "tried to tell herself that at least her kid had died for something. But a street sign's not much to die for."

Her voice did break then and she had to look away, out the window where, as she blinked back her tears, she could just see a corner of gray and brooding November sky. *Help me, Jon,* she prayed. *Don't let me mess this up.*

"Please," she said, unconsciously lifting her hands to the congregation as she turned back to them. "Please. At least let his death be worth something. Don't just throw him away. Please stop fighting, if not for yourselves, then for him."

After that, she didn't know what more to say or do, and for a minute no one in the congregation moved. Then the minister cleared his throat and said, "Let us all sing hymn number 347." He came toward her, but before he could reach her, Pippa was there, putting an arm around her, taking her hand.

Under cover of the hymn, Pippa led Kate back to her pew.

EPILOGUE

EVERYONE did stop fighting, but it was a long time before Kate was sure of anything again.

The feud stopped. Rab, under pressure from Jon's parents and his own, turned himself in and was sent to a juvenile rehabilitation center, and a two-town committee was formed to study the waste-plant question. Within a year, ground was broken for the plant in an isolated dry section of woods outside Warton, miles from the nearest house.

Kate learned to smile again, and even to laugh; she played with Cassie, who was in what seemed to be permanent remission; she went out with Nick; she ran with Pippa. But there was nothing, she found, that she could do to ease the ache inside.

I still don't understand, Mr. Pot, she said the day after her high school graduation, walking alone through the overgrown blueberry bushes to their frogging place. Cruelty, war, sadness—I still don't understand.

She knelt and gently cupped her hand around a tadpole, feeling its tiny body beat against her finger, struggling to be free. Blind instinct, she thought; he'd do anything to get away from me; he's terrified—and he can't think, can't reason. Can he feel, beyond the terror? Certainly not like a person.

But people *won't* feel, *won't* think. Why?

She opened her hand and let the tadpole go. It wriggled away, thrashing its thin tail against the ripples the breeze made.

"Questing, Mr. Pot," Kate said aloud, "for tadpole things."

She thought of the books, Jon's, her father's, Dan's —history, religion, psychology, music, philosophy, literature—stacked in her room near the forms she had to fill out for Harvard, where she'd be going in the fall. She hadn't found any answers in them, so far.

She watched the tadpole navigate around a leaf, a rock.

Quests aren't easy, Mr. Pot, are they?

You knew all along, didn't you?

"A quest, then, Mr. Pot," she said, aloud again, ignoring the tears that blurred her eyes. "Yours and mine." She stood. "Still with me?"

She turned toward the bridge to go home, and at last the ache began to subside.